I0570399

Dedicated to
Victoria Melita Hicks Philp

ACKNOWLEDGMENTS

Deep appreciation to poet Pol Hodge, General Secretary of the Cornish Language Fellowship, kernewek teacher, fierce language bard of Gorsedh Kernow, and a native of Redruth, Cornwall, for his infinite supply of wild and succinct Cornish swear words. I hope I have not mangled the language too badly.

Digging Too Deep

A Tosca Trevant Mystery

Jill Amadio

All rights reserved

Names, characters and incidents depicted in this book are products of the author's imagination or are used fictitiously. Any resemblance to actual events, organizations, or persons, living or dead, is entirely coincidental and beyond the intent of the author or the publisher.

No part of this book may be reproduced or transmitted in any form or by any means, electronic or mechanical, including photocopying, recording, or by any information storage and retrieval system, without permission in writing from the publisher.

Copyright © 2013 by Jill Amadio

ISBN: 978-1-7326560-0-0

Published in the United States of America

ONE

"Sorry I'm late, Mother. Have you been standing out here long? We had a death on the island, and the memorial service ran on forever," said J.J. Trevant. She picked up the two suitcases and loaded them into the Porsche parked curbside at Los Angeles International Airport.

"A murder? *Re'm fay!* Right on my new American doorstep." Tosca Trevant pursed her lips.

"No, of course not a murder. Where did you get that idea? A neighbor drowned. And what on earth do you mean, right on your doorstep?"

"I've put in for a promotion from gossip columnist to crime reporter, so I need a murder to solve. Don't be dense, dear."

J.J. slammed down the trunk lid and stared at Tosca. "That's ridiculous. You know nothing about crime writing. Besides, this wasn't a murder. The poor woman died on vacation in Mexico. Surely the royal scandal you discovered wasn't a crime, was it?"

"Let's not get into that right now, love."

J.J. opened the passenger door for her mother, who stepped in and buckled her seat belt.

"How was the flight?" asked J.J. as they drove out of the terminal. "That eleven-hour trip from London is no picnic. Did you sleep? It must have been horribly uncomfortable for you in that unbelievably short outfit."

"This?" Tosca tugged at the hem of her black leather miniskirt. "You've been out of England too long. Covers my knickers all right, doesn't it? The toddler I held on my lap part of the flight didn't mind. What a joy it was to cuddle him. You'll learn that when you have children of your own."

"Not on my radar, as you know."

Tosca sighed. "You can't race cars forever."

J.J. glanced at her mother. "And look at your hair! It's down to your waist now." She frowned. "Bit old for that, too, aren't you?"

"Old? I haven't said hello to fifty yet, although it's fast approaching. *Re'm fay.*"

"I wish you wouldn't swear in Cornish, Mother. It makes you sound more eccentric than you are. No offense, of course."

"None taken, love. I will try my best to behave myself. Apologies for descending upon you with hardly any warning. I was so rudely hustled out of England, I barely had time to send you those jugs of mead. I hope they didn't get too jostled en route. I can't wait to have a glass."

J.J. shrugged. "I haven't opened the box. You know I hate that awful plonk you insist on brewing yourself. Anyway, now that you're here you can relax."

Tosca raised her eyebrows. "Relax? With a royal lawsuit hanging over my head? Fat chance. I'm in exile."

"No, you're not. You've been reassigned, that's all. Don't exaggerate."

"I still can't believe I caused such an uproar." At J.J.'s snort, Tosca grimaced. "Honestly, I had no idea Queen Elizabeth would be so rattled. She should know my 'Tiara Tittle-Tattle' column is harmless."

"Harmless? Like a python. The royals never know where you'll strike next. That piece you wrote last week about the Earl of Dunene's false teeth falling into the queen's lap at dinner was a bit mean spirited, don't you think?

"But it was true! The footman told me he saw the earl try to catch them, but it was too late."

"All right, but you still haven't told me what your scoop was. Sex again, I suppose. Your last email said that you'd blundered through the wrong door at Buckingham Palace, and you'd be arriving here today. Sounds really bad, so tell me."

"It wasn't sex, for a change, and the palace hushed it up, of course. No, J.J., I've promised not to discuss it, even though it was the best scoop of my career. That wimpy editor Stuart assured the Queen's Counsel and their vast team of barristers and solicitors the column would never see the light of day. In exchange for my silence over what I saw, as I said, I asked Stuart to switch me to crime reporting, but he refused."

"Sorry, Mother, but I can't see you interviewing murderers and families of victims unless they're wearing crowns."

"I've always wanted to cover criminal cases for the newspaper, but I got stuck with the gossip column. Oh, well, at least I still have a job."

J.J. guided the car expertly onto the southbound 405 freeway, weaving in and out of six lanes of giant tanker trucks, semis and bumper-to-bumper traffic until the carpool lane appeared. She entered it and gunned the engine past eighty miles an hour.

"Goodness, dear!" Tosca clutched the armrests. "Don't you think you should slow down? We're not on one of your speedway tracks. I can't imagine why you chose such a dangerous career as racing. Too much like your father, God rest his soul."

"We'll be home soon. Please, just close your eyes."

Ignoring her daughter's advice, Tosca swiveled her head rapidly from side to side as she took in their surroundings on the drive south and kept up a running commentary.

"Look at that! Perfectly proportioned palm trees. Poor things. Not really their natural state, is it? And there's yet another McDonald's right near the ramp. Still, it's very convenient for drivers and, I hear, much better than our miserable motorway cafes and the greasy atomic depth-charges they claim are burgers. Oh, will we be passing that mangled spaceship they call Disney Hall? Looked a bit tortured in the photos I saw."

"No, it's downtown Los Angeles. Mother, you really should rest your eyes."

Arriving on Isabel Island after crossing the short bridge that connected it to the coastal town of Newport Beach, J.J. took Center Street, which cut through the island for three blocks. Lined with shaggy eucalyptus trees, it was the island's hub and heart with cafes, boutiques, small art galleries, craft stores and a tiny post office. During the summer Center Street teemed with tourists before they headed for the ferries, two fifty-seven-foot barges, to take them across to the four-mile-long peninsula on the other side of the harbor. Built in 1906, the ferries were a year-round fixture that carried passengers and three vehicles across the main channel every three minutes.

"Oh, this is delightful." Tosca sat up straighter. "It has a village atmosphere, almost like Cornwall. I think I'm going to like it here."

J.J. turned left onto Felton Drive, passing two policemen on bicycles.

"I feel at home already. Bobbies on bikes," said Tosca, waving and smiling at them.

"The island is mostly narrow, one-way streets, Mother. Believe me, it's much easier for the cops to ride their bicycles than maneuver cars around here."

She drove to the end of Felton, turned left, left again into a narrow alley and stopped in front of a garage beneath a two-story house. She pressed the door opener on the car's sun visor, drove in and parked.

"Here we are. My apartment is upstairs. We'll get you a rental car tomorrow. You'll only need it for a few days, then you can drive the Austin-Healey. Oh, don't groan like that. It's a really great car. A classic."

"Sixty years ago that old bucket may have been great, but the last time I sat in it, with your father behind the wheel, the seat bit my bum." At J.J.'s laugh Tosca added, "It's true. The gap between the seatback and the seat itself had widened. When I sat down, I got nipped."

They exited the Porsche and unloaded the suitcases. J.J. led the way up two flights of wooden steps that hugged the outside wall of the house and opened the Dutch door to the living room of her apartment.

"The bedrooms are up there." She pointed to a spiral staircase. "We can take the luggage up later. Cup of tea? I have all your favorites."

Tosca shook her head. "No thanks, love. I'm anxious to have a glass of mead. I made one of the recipes from sweet briar. It should have come out perfectly. Oh, roses!" Tosca turned toward the large floral display on the coffee table.

"Yes, Professor Whittaker gave them to me after the funeral service. It was his wife Monica who died."

TWO

Letter from a Lonely Outpost. *Hello, dear Reader. I have settled onto this lovely little island and will be ferreting out some delicious tidbits for you from this side of the Big Pond. I miss the Savoy and the Ritz bar terribly but have just discovered there is a Ritz right here, thank heavens, even though it is in the middle of a shopping mall where fashionistas are buying a new perfume called Gossip! An omen, perhaps? Someone here has written a 147-page poem. Took him forty years, and he says he doesn't completely understand it. Not surprising. Toodle-oo sweet Reader, till next time.*

Tosca thought about the neighbor's wife as she left J.J.'s apartment for her usual early morning walk. She found it difficult to reconcile the darkness of death when every day now was filled with sunshine.

After a week on Isabel Island, Tosca was in love with the balmy Southern California climate but still missed the frequent cloudbursts that freshened her English homeland.

As she strode briskly around the three-mile seafront, a folded parasol at the ready in her hand, she examined everything in sight with a suspicious eye. She'd given up counting the dozens of powerboats docked in the bay, the small boats bobbing on moorings and the expensive yachts berthed alongside private docks, matching the opulence of the chic beach houses crammed together like dominos in a box. Snow-clad mountains towered in the distance, dwarfing the gleaming white skyscrapers of Newport Beach's luxury hotels and office buildings.

But every day brought a new dilemma.

"What? No proper teashop nearby?" she'd protested to J.J.

Tosca glanced skyward as she walked. A-barth am Jowl! Not a drop of rain, either. As the sun lazily nudged itself over the hills and took its first look of the day at the wide Newport Beach harbor and the bay big enough to embrace seven small islands, Tosca opened the parasol to shade herself. She called out a cheerful "Good morning!" to a jogger as he passed. Foremost in her mind, though, was where to find the kind of gossip for her column from America that her editor, Stuart Prebble, demanded while she sought a crime to solve.

"Stuart, I don't think there's much royal gossip where I'm going, and certainly no authentic royalty. Can't I be an investigative reporter instead?" she'd asked for the fourth time before she left London.

Not that Tosca felt that the "Tiara Tittle-Tattle" column was beneath her, especially since she inevitably managed to ferret out private tidbits before anyone realized they'd revealed them. For eleven years she'd held her readers enthralled or appalled, depending on their sympathies toward the throne. That is, until she was rather swiftly banished, she complained, just like the exiled Duke of Windsor, who was booted to the Bahamas for marrying an American divorcee. Exalted company, indeed, but humiliating. She was grateful that *London Daily Post* readers knew nothing of the real reason for her reassignment. Tosca's farewell column was headlined, "Goodbye London, Hello Los Angeles." The new title was, "Tête-a-Tête with America."

When the editor called her into his office to tell her, she'd said, "Oh, for goodness sake, Stuart. That sounds fatuous, and what am I supposed to be writing about? How America takes tea? The Tea Partyers? Tête-a-Tête indeed. I think my reassignment is the perfect opportunity for a splendid new start. How about it?"

"No way, Tosca. We want readers to follow you across the pond for your impressions. What's it like living there? Tell me about some of those bizarre happenings that Americans take for granted, not the usual Hollywood celebrity trash. I want gossipy stories about real people. That makes you almost a news reporter, right?"

"Well, I'll give it a try. But promise me you'll work on our legal problem with the royals."

At first she'd told herself the threatened lawsuit was due to her description of the queen's latest appearance in that dreadful blue frock as "gravity having claimed her ample bosom." But of course she knew it was for the discovery she'd made, and the matter was far more serious than a mere criticism of the monarch's elderly figure.

Maybe now that J.J. is now a proud U.S. citizen I should become one, too, she reflected, and report on crimes on the West Coast. There seem to be plenty of shootings, judging by the media. I might never go back to England. Let the Brits solve their own murders.

But despite the beauty of the beach town in which she now resided, Tosca already missed the hustle and bustle of the London tube stations and their trains that ran underground all over the city. She missed the wild Cornish moors of her childhood that gave her respite on weekends in the country, and she missed the vibrant energy that millions of Londoners, speaking dozens of different languages and dialects, brought to the chattering streets. She even missed Buckingham Palace, although it had been her downfall. Would Queen Elizabeth really go through with the lawsuit? Well, I'll have to make the best of it, she decided.

"J.J.," she'd asked her daughter a day after her arrival, "where will I find *vino nero* among the hundreds of California brands?"

"That black Sardinian wine? You really must learn to adjust, Mother. Our Sonoma and Napa Valley wines are renowned worldwide. Here," said J.J., "try this *pinot noir*. I bought it especially for you."

After she tasted the wine Tosca admitted it was passable and even agreed that Orange County offered a tranquility and beauty that could be considered paradise. But as she strode along the seafront she thought about having to adjust to the conformity she was encountering in her new home.

A Starbucks on every corner. Stainless steel appliances in every kitchen, she'd heard. And as for the epidemic of fake breasts everywhere, as round as soccer balls and equally, she suspected, as hard, she had to admit the practice had found its way to Britain and been eagerly embraced.

Besides, who am I to judge? she told herself. Jolly old England isn't so jolly anymore, ever since the Beatles left center stage and Camilla came to town. *A-barth an Jowl,* Tosca swore. Now I'm complaining again. Well, this gorgeous place really is annoying, she thought. Not a breath of bloody wind, not a cloud in the sky. Oh, for a nice, wet drizzle, that soft, steady, misty rain that can last for hours and require the wearing of Wellies.

She walked past a pseudo-Tudor cottage slotted between two small Swiss-style chalets, taking a perverse delight in trying to decipher the island's eclectic housing styles. Along the bay's canals were Dutch colonials with overhanging eaves, Spanish-style stucco, adobes topped with red tiles and a Cape Cod built next to a couple of grand pseudo-haciendas. The mix of styles also included a handful of New England saltboxes and several large Georgian homes that stood on double lots, their formal stone sills and ornate roof balustrades completely out of place at the beach.

"Isabel Island's saving grace," she declared to J.J., "is its variety of architecture. I love it. It's a bizarre hodgepodge of styles. No conformity here, thank goodness. Of course, none of it is worth a brass farthing as far as elegance goes."

"How about our beautiful little front yards?" said J.J.

As she recalled her daughter's words, Tosca stopped in front of one of the houses, leaned over the owner's low garden wall, reached toward a rose bush and began snapping off dead flower heads. Finished with the task, she brushed aside fallen leaves from a nearby eucalyptus tree. Don't people know these trees are among the highest emitters of hydrocarbons, contributing to smog? she grumbled. And Americans have no idea how to grow roses. Then she remembered the many prizes they won at the annual Chelsea Flower Show. I'm testy because it's not raining, she told herself, and I'm bored. From a hotbed of royal intrigue to worrying about a bed of roses. What a comedown.

Tosca passed by the house of J.J.'s recently widowed neighbor, Professor Haiden Whittaker, giving it a quick glance before stopping and retracing her steps to his front gate. Yes, the garden was still a mess. Appalling. She'd noticed it yesterday and the day before that. The white picket fence was easy to see over, but she could barely make out the rock garden through the thick vegetation that covered it. Tucked into a corner of the yard against the west wall of the house, it was almost three feet in length, five feet high and built in the shape of a pyramid. Ah well, the poor man must still be grieving, she decided. Maybe I can help.

She approached the front door and rang the bell. After a few minutes she rang again. When no one answered, she marched across to the overgrown area in the corner.

"A disgrace," she muttered, pushing aside tall, scraggy weeds. "All this rock garden needs is tidying up. Hello, what's this? Good heavens, where on earth did he get the idea to put these big stones on top? They belong at the bottom. Foolish man. They must be ten inches around. Much too big."

Heavy, too, she thought, grunting as she picked one up. She noticed a small chunk had crumbled away, revealing four inch-long, stick-like objects embedded in the rock. How strange. Fossils? But as she touched them she felt a chill run through her. She had a sudden suspicion she knew what they were. Impossible. She replaced the rock and walked home. I absolutely refuse to worry about Professor Haiden Whittaker's weeds again or that strange stone they're hiding, she promised herself.

THREE

Letter from a Lonely Outpost. *Hello, dear Reader. Still no rain, so irritating. I am looking forward to a most amusing event, the Pasadena Doo-Dah Parade, where marchers wheel along their barbecues and hibachis, shopping carts and almost anything else on wheels. They're joined by a group called The Committee for the Right to Bear Arms, each one of the team carrying a mannequin's arm, I am told. Can you believe it, David Beckham and the adorable Posh abandoning Hollywood and moving to Paris? Probably the cheese. Toodle-oo, sweet Reader, till next time.*

"You know, J.J., that professor has no idea how ugly and neglected his garden is," Tosca said at breakfast the following day. *"Mab-mollowthow."* At J.J.'s raised eyebrows she explained, "It means he's cursed by his parents. He must be, considering the plight of those poor geraniums, but worst of all is that hideous rock garden stuck away in the corner. I took a good look at it. It's totally overgrown and topped by two of the weirdest rocks I've ever seen. One of them is very odd."

"I thought the whole idea of a rock garden was to include rocks," said J.J.

"In proper proportion, yes, but these are much too big, and they're round, like melons. You'd never see such imbalance in English gardens, as well you know. I'm going to have to ring his doorbell again and say something. He's a right twit."

"Maybe they're petrified melons," J.J. laughed, then shrugged. "Anyway, why are you so concerned about someone's garden? You're not a gardener. What's this new interest?"

"I'm curious, that's all. You know how I like to know things."

"Like to meddle, you mean. That's what got you into such trouble with the palace."

"You did say the professor lived alone, didn't you, now that he's a widower? I should bake him some scones and go over for tea."

"Mother, I'm warning you. It's different here. We don't just drop in on people for a cup of tea. Besides, he just lost his wife. Probably hasn't had time to work on his garden."

J.J. rose from the bench in the breakfast nook and refilled the milk jug. A shorter, more slender version of her mother with cropped brown hair framing her heart-shaped face, J.J. was wearing the T-shirt she'd slept in. Emblazoned on its front were a large number three and the name of her NASCAR race driver hero, Dale Earnhardt, who'd been killed in a crash during the Daytona 500.

"You said the professor's wife died suddenly?" asked Tosca.

"Yes, in the hotel pool. An accident. He had her cremated in Mexico and brought the ashes back home."

"Very sensible. I shall tell him so. I'd be cremated myself if it weren't so iffy."

"Iffy?"

"Remember that case in Scotland where the funeral director was arrested for only half-cremating the dead bodies to save on his energy bill? Claimed he was with Greenpeace. Now I must go and see Professor Whittaker. I really want to help him with his garden." And take a closer look at that stone, she added to herself.

"Oh, Mother, how can he think about something like that? He needs time to grieve and be alone."

"I know, I know. I wish you'd stop scolding me. You may be twenty-four years old and a race car champion, but I am still your mother. *Gas dha son,* for goodness sake."

"I am not nagging," said J.J.

"Aha! So you do remember your Cornish."

"Just a few phrases, although I think you are mixing up Unified Cornish with colloquialisms. Look, I'm sorry, Mother, but you must leave the neighbors alone."

"Once he takes a look at the weeds and realizes he's placed those peculiar rocks in the wrong place, especially the one that's broken apart, he'll appreciate my concern. It's probably pure ignorance on his part, that's all, even if he is a professor."

"He's a professor of music, not archaeology or geology or whatever the science is. You had no right to go into his garden."

"I only wanted to tidy it up, but when I took a close look at one of the rocks and saw four bony bits inside, I got shivers down my back."

"Fossils, probably. I bet the California desert's full of small round boulders like that."

"My dear girl, that's exactly what I thought, too, at first. Fossils. But I am positive that rock contains the top third of four skeletal human fingers. Someone has definitely popped their clogs. Dead as a doornail."

"Mother! That's an outrageous thing to say!"

"Oh, yes indeed. I am very suspicious. There's something funny going on. I'm telling you that they are the tips of human fingers."

At least I hope they are, added Tosca to herself. Please let them be part of a human skeleton, and please, Lord, forgive me, but just imagine the headline, "Tosca Solves Murder in America," and my byline, "Tosca Trevant, Crime Reporter." Then I could go home in triumph and be an investigative reporter. I know most of the senior chappies at Scotland Yard, a couple of MI6 agents and dear old Jonathan, the MI5 director-general at Thames House. Then, of course, there's Stan, the security director for Buckingham Palace's police division. I've become quite chummy with him since the scandal.

"I definitely smell a rat in that garden," Tosca said, "and I don't mean that's what those bones are."

J.J. rolled her eyes. "They're probably claws from an eagle or a hawk. Maybe bear claws. You're being melodramatic."

"Oh, stop getting your knickers in a twist. I know what I saw. The bones look like some I've seen in morgues and in your grandfather's medical clinic. You know I took a course in forensics. All right, so it was only a two-hour seminar, but I learned a lot. I've decided to visit your neighbor later today, at tea time."

"Mother dear, do stop being so English. We don't have that four o'clock ritual here, remember?"

"Indeed I do remember, and I still think it's a disgrace. You know, J.J., you didn't have to abandon your heritage when you became an American citizen." Tosca glanced at the clock. Ten past nine. "As a matter of fact this is an even better time to call on him. The early bird catches the worm." She rose and took the breakfast dishes over to the sink.

"I don't want you getting up to your old tricks again," said J.J. to her mother's back. "You promised me your days of digging up dirt on people were on hold. Fortunately, that weekly column you're sending to the *London Daily Post* about your impressions of America isn't read here. The last thing we need is unnecessary gossip, especially since you'll be staying for a whole year."

"I never write unnecessary gossip, dear child. That's a contradiction in terms. My gossip columns are all documented and corroborated," Tosca laughed, "except for the last one, of course. Pity it was so scandalous that it won't see the light of day. I quite like the prince."

"I don't see why. You said he was the one responsible for orchestrating what you call your exile and probably the lawsuit."

"Yes, it distresses me, but at least the gossip columns Stuart wants are easy, sort of a here-I-am-in-the-crazy-colonies type of approach. I'm already doing research. Did you know that the Beverly Hills post office provides valet parking for its customers, and the Newport City Hall has a wine bar?"

"So what? Brings in pretty good revenue."

"I'll concede that, but what about that boutique on Center Street called Altitude? I went in yesterday to buy a GPS update and found myself talking to a salesgirl's bosom. She towered over me, must be six feet five, at least. I must admit the name is a very clever play on words, but not a GPS in sight."

J.J. shook her head, laughing. "Of course not. It's clothing for tall ladies. As you can imagine, I've never gone inside."

"Maybe it's a good item for my new column. I read a really outrageous bit in the *Los Angeles Times* about the Los Angeles Opera commissioning a work based on the sounds heard along the motorways here. Imagine! Honking horns, squealing brakes and police sirens. Hardly melodic. Still, I think that's the kind of bizarre behavior Stuart wants in my new column."

Tosca whistled a couple of notes as she continued to clear off the breakfast table.

"When did you take up whistling, Mother? You don't do it very well, and you're spraying all over the place."

"I know. It helps me stop thinking about why I had to leave home. I love you dearly, child, but I sorely miss my *tre*."

"I assume *tre* means home?"

"Of course it does, J.J." Tosca sat down again, resting her arms on the table. "You used to speak Kernewek perfectly when you first learned to talk."

"Well, it's all forgotten," said J.J. "I bet I never spoke it at all after we left Cornwall to live in London."

The mention of London reminded Tosca of the scene she'd come across upstairs at Buckingham Palace and the threat of the lawsuit. It has uprooted my life, she thought, ruined my career, and not a single colleague, not even Stuart, has really stood by me. I feel completely betrayed and abandoned. I don't belong there, and I don't belong here either.

Suddenly, she put her head down on her arms and began to weep.

"Mummy!" said J.J., reverting to her childhood name for her mother. "What on earth's the matter?" She put her arms around Tosca's shoulders as her mother continued to sob. She took some tissues from the box on the table and gave them to her. Finally, Tosca stopped crying and raised her head.

"Oh, J.J., you're crying, too. I'm sorry to worry you. It's the lawsuit, of course. It really is getting me down." She passed the box of tissues to her daughter. "Stuart says in his email today that it's far more serious than we thought."

"I've never seen you cry before," said J.J. "It frightens me."

Tosca tried to laugh. "Here we are, two modern women people think are so tough, you on the race track and me out there bashing the mighty monarchy, and all we can do is sit here and bawl like babies." She stood up. "Tea. That'll do the trick. No, forget the tea. Dry your tears, *keresik*. I am determined to beard the professor in his den and ask about those rocks I dug up."

She hurried up the spiral staircase to the two small attic bedrooms under the arched roof. Light and airy, their windows offered a glimpse of the main channel that connected boaters to the back bay, but like all the other houses on Isabel Island, J.J.'s home sat cheek-by-jowl with its neighbors, huddled together with only inches, it seemed, between the narrow lots.

As Tosca changed clothes her soprano voice filled the air.

"Mother!" J.J. shouted up the stairs. "I told you. Do not burst into those arias of yours while you're here, especially not that screechy *Madame Butterfly*. You can be heard all over the island. You know how closely together we live, and we're very respectful of each other's privacy."

"How can you say that about *Madame Butterfly?*" Tosca shouted back as she broke off in mid-note. "Cio-Cio San was the sweetest, gentlest lady in the history of opera. No one can possibly object to hearing 'One Fine Day.' Besides, it's not considered truly grand opera, so why the fuss? Just be glad I don't like that tyrant Wagner."

Ten minutes later she floated down the spiral staircase wearing an ivory and blue flowered silk dress, her long, dark hair gathered into a bun at the nape of her neck.

"I still wish you wouldn't go bothering the professor," said J.J. "I don't trust you an inch when you get that look in your eye. You must stop studying Americans as if they were prize specimens, and must you carry that ridiculous parasol? This is the twenty-first century, not the eighteenth."

"It just doesn't feel right to go outside without an umbrella. I never did in England."

"Everyone needs one there. It's always raining."

"I love this parasol. Its little Chinese cherries are so cheerful. Of course, I could wear my red hat instead, the one that perches over my right eye like the ones Kate and Pippa Middleton wear, although now that Kate's married to Prince Wills she has to keep her hats off the face, like the queen."

J.J. groaned.

Tosca raised her hands in silent defense.

"All right, no hat. Now look, that man needs my help. The poppies are falling over, and those hollyhocks are far too tall for the size of his garden. It's a complete shambles." To say nothing of someone's finger bones in a rock, she thought.

"I hope you're not taking any of that god-awful mead with you," called J.J. as her mother slammed the front door behind her.

FOUR

Letter from a Lonely Outpost. *Hello, dear Reader. My favorite actor, John Cleese, is living along the California coast in Santa Barbara so I'll be seeing him soon, such a delicious man...reading the newspapers here is a revelation in modernity, so many vowels simply tossed away in favour of brevity (all the 'u' letters have disappeared)...impossible to find mead anywhere, blank stares when I ask...very odd that Americans haven't caught on to the metric system yet so one must endlessly convert measurements and degrees. Rather confusing...All for now, dear Reader. Toodle-oo till next time.*

Tosca snapped the parasol closed, hooked it onto her arm, pushed the white picket gate wide open and entered Professor Whittaker's garden. Overgrown crimson hibiscus vines and wild roses intertwined the latticework of the arbor leading to the front door. Scarlet bougainvillea, not yet in full bloom, cascaded from the home's low roof. Who grows flowers on his roof? she wondered. Crazy Californians.

Two pygmy date palm trees stood sentinel as Tosca picked her way carefully along the narrow flagstone path edged with purple and canary-yellow pansies that nodded gently in the warm Pacific breeze. When she reached the rock garden she picked up the broken stone and approached the front door.

White plantation shutters partially shielded the front windows from the morning sun. Between the half-open slats Tosca could easily make out the bulky form of the professor completely filling an oversized, high-backed, red leather armchair. It was turned toward the bay and the twin jetties that marked the harbor entrance. Behind him, angled to his right, she saw a grand piano and sheet music on its holder.

Tosca hesitated as she noted he was still in his bathrobe, engrossed in reading a newspaper. His head was bent down to reveal strands of gray hair carefully combed and judiciously spaced to cover the bald spots.

It's simply got to be done, Tosca told herself as she found the bell and pressed it firmly. Judging the music professor to be a sensitive soul, she kept her eyes modestly away from the sight of him in his chair in case he jumped up in fright at the shrill sound of the bell that reverberated through the glass-paneled door. She turned toward the bay to take in the full beauty of her surroundings. By now she was used to the splendor of the yachts tied up to docks that extended like spokes in a wheel around the perimeter of the peaceful island, but she still marveled at the variety of lilies, irises, roses, dahlias and geraniums that bloomed, it seemed, all winter.

"Yes?"

She whipped around at the professor's terse greeting.

"Ah. Yes. How charming of you to answer the door. I'm terribly sorry to disturb you on a Sunday morning, and isn't it gorgeous, but I did want to catch you in, you see." Barely pausing for breath while the man's frown lines deepened as he glanced at the rock in her hands, Tosca continued. "I know we haven't been properly introduced, but being neighbors, one can't help but notice. I'm Tosca Trevant. I'm visiting my daughter, J.J.," she pointed, "two doors away."

Whittaker looked at her blankly but offered no reply. Tosca plunged on. "You must have seen or at least heard J.J. driving madly around in that little red sports car of hers? Not the Porsche. I mean the British one, the 1953 Austin-Healey BN1 open top. Quite rare. Her father left it to her when he died, and she shipped the dreadful old banger over here. Imagine owning three cars. How American! She keeps the Porsche for rallying next to the Healey in the garage, and her NASCAR race car is with the team, of course. I do ask her to slow down on these one-way streets, but being a race car driver, she won't listen to anyone. I wish she'd get a proper job. She drove like a maniac in England and does the same here. Our London traffic, of course, is dreadful, but we have such wonderfully frequent trains and buses. Very clean they are, too. In fact, some are actually immaculate, especially the Orient Express from London, and..."

"What do you want?" The voice was high-pitched and querulous. He stroked the bristly, meticulously barbered mutton-chop whiskers that book-ended his cheeks.

"This is a most peculiar request, but can you tell me about your, um, beautifully kept garden?" She indicated the area where she'd found the broken rock and wilting plants. "I realize that terraced part of the garden has been there for quite some time, judging by its condition. Was it in place when you bought the house?"

Thud. The glass panels quivered as the door slammed shut. Well, outrageous! And extremely rude, decided Tosca. Here I am in my Sunday best, as polite as could be, and he slams the door in my face. Before she could turn away the door swept open again.

"Sorry, Mrs. Trevant. My wife's death, you see..."

Professor Whittaker's fleshy cheeks puffed out in a smile that radiated insincerity. He extended a pale, plump hand.

"Please accept my condolences, Professor, and do call me Tosca," she said, resting the rock against her chest with one hand and shaking his hand with her other, quickly rescuing her crushed thumb. In spite of a flabby appearance, Whittaker's grip was iron.

"I am a widow myself," she said, "so I can appreciate how you feel. If I'm a bother, just let me know. However, there is definitely something wrong in your garden. Here, I've brought you the culprit." She held up the rock.

"My garden?" Whittaker took a few steps down the path and glanced around to the back corner.

"Ah, yes, you think so, too. Your eyes went straight to the problem. So I am right. It's those interesting stones on top. Take a look at this one."

"Let's talk inside." The professor's black silk bathrobe flapped around pudgy ankles as he turned abruptly back into the house, his short, quick steps revealing matching pajamas.

Tosca followed him, thinking she had rarely encountered a more globular man. He seemed to be made up of a series of circles. Head like a Halloween pumpkin topped with strands of hair like wet string, sitting on a neckless spherical torso, and a rotund belly that Tosca guessed must be attached to fat, bulbous legs.

Yet, she realized, his face had once been handsome with velvety brown eyes, a well-defined Roman nose he held slightly up in an arrogant tilt, and wide, sensuous lips. But the heavy jowls almost enveloped his chin, and his lower cheeks had long since drowned in a river of indulgence.

Haiden Whittaker's long living room was crowded with 19th century antique armoires; mahogany side tables, and a red velvet Victorian sofa pushed against the far wall, all genuine pieces except for the red leather armchair, guessed Tosca, who was familiar with Buckingham Palace's magnificent treasures. There seemed no plan to the room's arrangement, as if someone had simply removed the furniture from their packing boxes years ago and left them where they stood. Only the ebony piano shone with polish.

Scattered over almost every surface and much of the floor were stacks of sheet music, blank score pages and CDs. Tosca was not totally surprised to see several sheets ripped to shreds. She figured that the professor, like other composers, often tore up his ideas in rage and frustration.

Lined up along the mantel above the brick fireplace was a collection of nine small, crudely fashioned sculptures resembling different sizes and shapes of what appeared to be animal paws. What on earth are those? wondered Tosca, comparing their clumsy design to the rest of the room's elegant décor.

Whittaker cleared a space on the sofa. "Sorry about the mess. Please call me Haiden."

She noticed that like many large people, he barely moved when he talked, keeping gestures to a minimum. Tosca sat down, careful not to knock over the piles of magazines and books at her feet. She placed the rock on top of a newspaper on the coffee table.

"Now, tell me how I can help you," Whittaker said. "Your first name intrigues me, I must admit, being an opera lover."

Whittaker's brown eyes flicked from Tosca's face to her feet, to the piano and back to Tosca's hands.

He hasn't even glanced at the rock, she realized.

"My name? It's simple," she said. "My mother's relatives were all from Malta, and several of the men were opera singers. Two became members of the Carl Rosa Opera Company in England. My father was a Cornishman from St. Ives, but my mother insisted on naming us after opera characters. My name should really be Floria, as you know, not Tosca."

"Of course. Tosca was her last name."

"When my father went to the registry office and explained about the opera, he thoroughly confused the registrar, who made the same mistake as most people and mixed it up." Tosca smiled self-consciously.

As the professor's ponderous head nodded slowly in agreement, she wondered if the aroma of sandalwood she smelled was from incense, though Professor Whittaker hardly seemed the type. Had he been burning candles? If so, their fragrance failed to cover the fusty staleness in the room.

"In fact," he continued, "your name should be La Tosca, that's the title of the original play. But you've dropped your family's tradition of using an opera character's name for your daughter?"

"Not at all. J.J. was christened Joan after Verdi's heroine in his opera, *Joan of Arc*. It was his seventh and, as I'm sure you'll agree, one of his least popular compositions. I was willing to overlook the fact that Joan of Arc defeated the English, as we in Cornwall consider ourselves, even though we are a duchy, because I fell in love with the overture's woodwind solos and, of course, I admire Joan of Arc's incredible courage."

"Which your daughter now displays on the race track, as my late wife told me," said Whittaker. "However, what's all this about the stones in my front yard?"

Tosca looked out of the window at the shimmering bay where sea lions clustered on the platform around the huge main buoy, sunning themselves. On the sand dozens of families sat under blue and white beach umbrellas, enjoying their Sunday. At the water's edge a young couple, the girl in a yellow neon string bikini, laughingly toasted each other with champagne in red plastic glasses, spilling drops over their tanned bodies as they emptied the bottle.

"Yes, those two huge, round stones on top of your rock garden. There's something wrong with one of them. Surely you've noticed these four stick-like things here inside the broken-off part? They could be human bones. Four fingertips."

"Oh, I'm sure that's not true." The professor's eyes held hers. "Probably some animal. You're obviously not familiar with our desert kangaroo rat or the kit fox. Really, you're letting your imagination run away with you."

"On the contrary, professor. I am positive of my opinion. My father was a ship's surgeon in the Royal Navy during World War II. His clinic at home was jammed with specimen jars and bone fragments. Believe me, those things look very much like the skeletal tips of someone's fingers, though how they got stuck inside this small boulder, whatever it is, I can't imagine. In addition, your hardscape is out of proportion for a rock garden that height. Now don't you think we should notify the police?"

"The police?" Whittaker's voice shot up an octave. He stroked his whiskers as a flush spread over his face.

"It's the sensible thing to do," said Tosca.

"But I've already told you I know nothing about them. Perhaps they're American Indian remains. Don't worry, Tosca. There's nothing sinister going on here, believe me. Fingers embedded in rocks? Ridiculous. As for the hollyhocks and poppies, I'll take a look, as you suggest."

"I hope you do, professor. Hollyhocks are pretty tough plants, but they do need some pampering, a little *cara.*"

"What's that?"

"Oh, sorry. It's a Cornish word. It means love," said Tosca.

"Cornish? That's a language? I had no idea."

"Perfectly understandable, Haiden. Too many Brits don't know it either. In fact, the United Nations has declared our language dead, but we are going to fight against that. I am proud to declare we are the second smallest of the six Celtic nationalities. Cornwall is a duchy, but we're going to change that, too. We are preparing a legal challenge to the UK government. We want a return to self-rule, you see."

"Self-rule?"

"Indeed, yes. We were self-governed in 1508 as a separate Celtic nation. We've already established a fund and have our own flag, a white cross on a black background. Not terribly elegant, of course. I'd much prefer a pastel background and a more creative symbol, but the cross is traditional, you see."

She felt herself bristle when she saw the professor trying to hide a smile as he said, "Tosca, isn't 1508 rather a long time ago? I suppose your new champion is Camilla, the Duchess of Cornwall?"

Tosca drew her lips together in disapproval. "Not at all. Rather unfortunate, that alliance to the British monarchy. We pay seven million pounds a year toward Prince Charles' and Camilla's keep, you know. The money comes from Cornwall's surplus assets. Our attitude might have been different if Camilla wasn't just a token Cornishwoman." Tosca stood up, reaching for her purse and parasol. "I must be off. Thank you for your hospitality. Oh, one more thing. That purple lobelia plant in your yard? Not for salads. It can cause seizures. Good day, professor."

FIVE

Letter From a Lonely Outpost. My dear, dear Reader. The most extraordinary situation has occurred. I have found a skeleton, or rather, one of its hands...Now you know I love this gossip column and all of you, dear Readers, but for the moment I must say farewell...I am hot on the trail of a murder, absolutely no doubt about it...but you are always in my thoughts...I hope you will follow my newspaper stories as soon as the murderer is under lock and key and I have solved the mystery. Toodle-oo for a while, dear Reader.

As Whittaker recalled his conversation with Tosca after she left, he could still hear himself protesting, his heart pounding. He wasn't used to being challenged. Early on, his married life with Monica had settled into a monastic mode. For many years they barely had even conversational contact, moving about the house intent on their different schedules and only occasionally meeting up for dinner, with hardly a word passing between them. Their final meal together had been the most animated they'd had in a long time, he remembered with pleasure.

Damn that Tosca woman. Why was she snooping around? She said at first it was the hollyhocks that needed to be staked, but she sure as hell nailed the small shrine. Well, maybe he'd laid her suspicions to rest. She seemed to accept his explanation that he knew nothing about the construction of the corner area. It was there when he moved in, he told her.

Whittaker thought over their conversation once more. Had she bought his explanation about the garden?

Maybe he should just cement over the entire thing and fill it with potted plants.

Besides, as he'd told Monica before she died, it was getting close to the time to cash it all in now that he was almost sixty-five years old. He'd risen as high as he knew he could at the University of California, Irvine, becoming one of the most respected composers of classical music in the region. Yeah, well, that wasn't exactly the truth, he admitted to himself. In fact, it was a far cry from the truth. His latest compositions had been pure crap.

When had the music stopped playing in his mind? It had been subtle, the motifs and phrases fading away so gradually he'd barely missed them. He'd always assumed his gift was like Mozart's, who said he simply wrote down what he heard in his head. Whittaker thought he'd always hear the music, too, or rather, the idea of the music. Now the ideas were nonexistent, and the notes were a jumble.

Whittaker feared he was burned out. In his heart of hearts he knew that his latest arrangements were mechanical. He remembered reading a letter Tchaikovsky had written, lamenting that when inspiration deserted him he would fill in the blanks later. Blanks are all I have now, he thought, and maybe there is no later, but is that so bad? The sheet music royalties continue to swell the bank balance, and the pension is ample.

He sensed, though, that Tosca Trevant wasn't as satisfied as she claimed. There was a canny quality in those penetrating blue eyes that disturbed him. She also had a haughty air that was irritating. Hard to believe she was that girl's mother. They'd look more like sisters, if their clothes were similar. Nice to see a woman in a pretty dress for a change, and that quaint parasol! Monica would have hooted her off the island. Most of all, Tosca reminded Whittaker of the three fast and furious opening *tutta forza* chords of the opera she was named after: full force. The woman came on strong, all right. Whittaker patted his belly. No chance she'd be interested in me, not that I care. I'm off women forever. Pretty little hands, though. Very feminine.

Haiden tightened the sash of his silk bathrobe as the moon-dial grandfather clock struck noon. Monica used to make him get dressed first thing every morning, even on a Sunday. Now he wondered how he had ever let her control him like that.

He carried the rock outside and replaced it on top of the rock garden, turning its crumbled side toward the wall. Damned woman, he fumed. How dare she come into my yard and criticize? On the other hand, why hadn't I noticed the deterioration and taken better care of the shrine? I'd better do something with these two rocks before she returns.

Back in the house he sat down at the piano. He struck a match to light the black candle that stood in the center of a large brass bowl. As he pounded out the opening bars of Liszt's chilling "Danse Macabre," the flame flickered slightly with the vibration.

"Are you enjoying the candlelight you disliked so much?" he whispered, looking at the bowl. He suddenly stopped playing to give the candle a vicious twist, spilling a shower of ashes and tiny white pellets onto the piano keys.

"Did Haiden throw you out? What do you think of him?" asked J.J. when Tosca arrived home.

"He's odious. Said he had no idea about that rock, and there were no expressions of sorrow when I offered condolences about his poor wife. Another thing. When he smiles you never see his teeth."

"So what?"

"There are eighteen different kinds of smiles. The professor's smile meant he didn't wish to get acquainted."

"Beats baring his teeth in a snarl, I suppose," said J.J., laughing.

"Tell me. What's your impression of him since you've been living here?"

J.J. paused to reflect. "I guess, not too friendly. Monica, on the other hand, was pretty outgoing, but no one really likes her husband. Besides, he always buys the wrong car."

"The wrong car?"

"When Cadillac came out with the Seville," J.J. said, "Haiden bought the model without the Northstar V-8 engine. Then he bought a Jaguar XJS instead of waiting four months for the XK8, though how he squeezes into it, I can't imagine. Can't trust anyone who does something like that."

"Oh, come on, love. Get your mind off cars and driving for five minutes. We're talking about a possible killer on the loose."

"Mother! That's a huge leap from fossils in a rock to a killer on Isabel Island. This is the safest place on the West Coast. A bicycle stolen from a garage. Some fraud cases, too. After all, Newport Beach has been called the white collar scam capital of the country, but it's good, clean crime. Nothing messy."

Tosca filled the electric kettle at the faucet, plugged it in and turned back to her daughter.

"The professor suggests that those weird things in the rock that I'm convinced are human bones might be from some ancient American Indian burial site. Tea, dear?"

"Thanks, but no time. I'm rallying, for a change. Then tomorrow it's practice at the track." J.J., in jeans and a T-shirt, her short dark hair covered by a baseball cap, picked up the red and white racing helmet from the coffee table, blew her mother a kiss and left. A few seconds later she re-entered the house. "Hey!" she called out. "Will you stop calling those things bones?"

J.J. closed the door after her and clattered down the wooden steps to the garage. Barely a minute later Tosca heard the rumble she'd learned to recognize as the Porsche 911 Targa. The growl from its turbo engine filled the air, rose to a wail, then faded as the car headed across the island's only bridge.

Tosca carried her tea tray up to the roof deck and sat on one of the white patio chairs, looking around at the nearby homes. A seagull swooped down and settled on top of a telephone pole to her right. "This place is too perfect," Tosca complained to the bird. "Hasn't rained since I got here."

At twilight Tosca decided to take along her tote bag on her usual walk, which was more of a stroll than the brisk march she enjoyed at dawn. The slower pace gave her the chance to appreciate the scent of the small white flowers of the night-blooming jasmine in the several gardens she passed. On her approach to Haiden's house she noted that no lights showed from his windows. It appeared deserted. She looked up and down the street. No one. Should I chance it and see if he's replaced that spooky rock? she wondered. The houses on either side and across the way were also dark. Was everyone off at a rock concert? Hardly the taste of Isabel Island's elderly residents, but who knew what went on in Americans' minds after dark. She'd noticed a few tottering hippies, leftovers from 1960s Woodstock, she assumed, who were regulars at the local corner pub.

Taking a chance on the professor being out for the evening, Tosca pushed the gate open and walked to the back wall to see if the broken rock was still on top of the rock garden, though obviously he still hadn't weeded. Yes, there it was. Guess he's not too concerned about anyone taking more than a passing interest in it, she thought, even after I told him about the possibility of fingers inside it. Tosca bent down and hefted the heavy stone into her tote bag. She looked around again. Had anyone seen her? Apparently not. She hurried home.

The top half of the Dutch door was open. As she climbed to the top of the stairs she heard music and laughter. A gleaming silver trophy sat on the glass table, surrounded by racing helmets.

"We're celebrating, Mother. We won the Targa Triple Crown today. Stephen, Sandy and Mike, meet my mother."

"Delighted to meet you," said Tosca, shaking hands with all three of J.J.'s friends after leaving the tote bag on the kitchen counter. "Congratulations. Well done. One more to add to the collection."

"Thanks. J.J.'s trophy case is almost full already," said Mike, indicating the five-shelved cabinet in the corner of the room.

Tosca looked around at the lively faces. She decided they were an intelligent bunch of young people. She picked up her tote bag.

"May I show you all something and get your opinion?" She removed the heavy stone from the bag. Pointing to the thin sticks, she asked what they thought they were. The three crowded around, peering closely at the objects.

"Animal claws," said Sandy.

"Petrified wood chips," said Stephen.

"I've seen human skeletons. Their fingers look something like those things. They could be just the tips," said Mike

"Aha!" exclaimed Tosca. "That's what I think, too. Fingertips! But whose?"

"Mother, you see conspiracies everywhere." J.J. turned to her friends. "Mike, I'm sure you're wrong, and so is my mother. Come on, everyone, there's still some champagne left."

"But," said Tosca, "don't you think these belong to someone? Perhaps there was a murder. Imagine, right here! If those really are fingers, then the rest of the body must be around somewhere."

Tosca heard a snort from J.J. and turned to see the warning in her daughter's eyes: Don't meddle, Mother. Remember why your curiosity forced you to leave England.

SIX

Professor Whittaker stood in front of his rock garden, surveying its condition. When he first came up with the idea, he was keen to build one that was classic in appearance and plantings. He bought books on the subject, talked to colleagues at UC Irvine and visited garden centers.

"What kind of rocks and plants do I need for a garden on Isabel Island? Does being surrounded by water make a difference?" he asked a salesman at the local nursery.

Whittaker was eager to create exactly the right setting for the two precious trophies with which he planned to crown the rock garden's summit. He learned that the traditional elements included the construction of vertical ledges with small, low-lying, hardy plants such as white alyssum, pink phlox, Persian candytuft and purple lobelia. He bought gravel and special soil mixes that the salesman recommended.

But halfway through the project he became weary of trying to figure out how to place the various materials. He hired a gardener to set everything up. When it was finished, Whittaker waited until the man had been paid and driven off before installing the two treasures at the rock garden's highest point.

After its completion he enjoyed seeing it every time he left and returned to the house. He never observed Monica, of course, looking that way or mentioning it. Surely, she must have known and wondered. But after a few years, when he'd stopped caring for the shrine, and it was covered in crabgrass and other weeds, he'd almost forgotten it existed or, indeed, what it symbolized. Success and burgeoning celebrity meant more travel. During the summer months on hiatus from the university, he often spent weeks away, and he knew it never occurred to his wife to do any gardening.

Everything was going so well, "or it was until Mrs. Busybody Trevant came along," he muttered between clenched teeth, sweating with exertion under the noonday sun as he attacked the heavy growth of weeds he'd ignored for so long. He pulled back the alyssum that obscured the focus of the shrine and saw that one of the rocks was missing. With a curse he grabbed the remaining rock, scattering dirt as he pulled it free, and took it into the kitchen.

As Haiden stood at the stainless steel sink, gently washing off the soil and worrying about the other rock, the sound of grinding gears brought his glance up to window. He watched Tosca fling open the driver's side door of her daughter's Austin-Healey, jump out and stalk, red-faced, into their cottage. J.J., with a grim expression on her face, slid from the passenger seat, got behind the steering wheel and drove off, tires smoking. Here end-eth driving lesson number one, Whittaker thought as he recalled Tosca telling him she'd never learned to drive a manual transmission, but her daughter would teach her during her visit here.

The professor dried the rock, wrapped it in a kitchen towel and placed it in the bottom of the hall closet. Where was the other one in which Tosca had taken such an interest? Had she turned it over to the police? If so, what should he do? He forced himself to calm down. He'd told her the rock garden had been there when he moved in. Who could prove otherwise? The former elderly owners had moved to North Dakota. Probably dead by now.

Newport Beach Police Officer Andy MacAulay sat bolt upright in J.J.'s living room. "And where did you find this rock, ma'am?" he asked, still annoyed that the woman had practically pulled him off his bicycle ten minutes earlier and insisted he and his partner Bob come home with her to discuss a murder.

Assigned to patrol the island in pairs, on two wheels instead of four, the young cops enjoyed their bicycle duty. They even grinned at the friendly wolf whistles prompted by their uniforms of navy blue shorts and golf shirts. But occasionally, like today, Andy and his partner were presented with some weird situations.

"Where did I find it? Oh, at Professor Whittaker's house." Tosca waved her arm vaguely toward the street. "It was in his garden."

Taking the lead as his partner remained silent, Andy said, "I see. Did your neighbor give the rock to you?"

"Of course not," said Tosca.

"You mean, you went in and took it? That's trespassing, ma'am."

"Young man, do I look the type of person who would trespass?"

"Look, it's just a stone with a piece broken off one side," he said, anxious to leave.

He picked up the heavy, pinkish-gray lump Tosca had deposited in his lap and passed it over to Bob, who weighed it in his hand and gave it back to Andy. "It's very nice, ma'am. Should make a fine paperweight." He placed the rock on the table, wondering what she found interesting about the piece of rubble.

"But what about those fingertip bones?" said Tosca. "You must have this thing, whatever it is, X-rayed straight away. I've read all about America's advanced technology that can see inside anything. Failing that, just hit it with a hammer, but don't break those bones."

Andy decided to humor her. He'd ask the usual questions to show his willingness to help and then get out of there. Maybe he wouldn't even have to file a formal report.

"You said you are here visiting with your daughter?"

"Yes."

"I need your full name."

"Tosca Trevant."

"How old are you, Mrs. Trevant?"

"I beg your pardon?"

Jeez, just like my dad, he reflected, never wants to give away his age. "Ma'am, if you want me to fill out the report..." Andy held his pen poised over his notebook.

"Just write, 'unknown.'"

"Mrs. Trevant, maybe I could see your driver's license?"

"I haven't applied for a U.S. one yet."

"You're not driving, then?" said Andy, noting her guilty expression.

"I do have an international driver's license."

"Oh. That's all right then," he said, relieved enough to forget to ask her to produce it. He told her they'd take the rock with them for examination and asked her to walk with them past the professor's house to point out exactly where she'd found it.

"Before we've had tea? It's four o'clock!"

He watched her march into the kitchen, every angle of her body trembling with indignation, he figured, at his lack of respect for a fine English tradition. She grabbed the electric kettle, filled it at the faucet and slammed it back onto its heating base. The two policemen rolled their eyes at each other and signaled they'd better stay.

Andy fidgeted as he looked around the room. He studied the exotic Gauguin prints that covered one entire wall, the tall, thin abstract sculptures that reached to the ceiling, the racing trophies, and wondered what the daughter was like. Her mother looked great, but that formal way of speaking like some grand duchess unsettled him. Guess that how some Brits speak, he told himself. Suddenly, Tosca was at his elbow, a cup of tea clattering in its saucer. "Drink this. It's Oolong from Indonesia, much better than the Chinese. You, too," she said, handing Bob a cup.

They dutifully drank the hot liquid down.

"More?" asked Tosca.

"No, thanks, ma'am," said Andy. "I just need you to show us exactly where you found this thing, and then we'll be off."

On the street he unzipped the saddlebag at the rear of his bicycle, placed the rock inside, and reclosed the bag.

"Young man, you should put that into an evidence bag."

"Yes, ma'am."

The three made their way to Professor Whittaker's garden, the cops wheeling their bicycles and trying to avoid being poked in the eye by Tosca's parasol. As they walked along the street the policemen found themselves subjected to a stream of gossip and opinions.

"See this house?" said Tosca. "It's designed in four different architectural styles. You'd never see that in England, of course. That couple we just passed? They hate ducks. He blows them off his porch with a vacuum cleaner hose. Frightens them to death. They'll never be able to breed, you know. What do you think about that?"

Andy, who'd tried to tune out before the conversation overwhelmed him, began to reply, but the woman at his side sailed right on.

"Mrs. Jensen on the corner there hides her valuables all around the house. She drew up a schematic so she knows where everything is, but she keeps it in plain sight, pinned to the kitchen door. Her husband made his millions transforming defective coffins into fancy sofas."

Tosca pointed up the street. "See the little hole at ground level in the front wall of that house? Looks like a cat door, doesn't it? Well, it's not. The owner, Dick, loves toy trains. Every two hours his little engine pulling six carriages comes whistling out of the hole, takes a turn around the rose bush and chugs back inside." She grabbed Andy's arm. "Now just look at these two scrawny women jogging toward us. A man wants to feast on meat at night, not skinny things like them. Shocking, I call it. Of course, I hate to admit it but it's worse in England."

Andy decided that failing eyesight must be distorting her vision of the two beauties jogging past. Boy, so many gorgeous women, so little time. The parasol nicked his ear.

"My daughter won't let me have a proper umbrella around here, you know. That's why I carry this thing. She's trying to talk me into one of those fold-ups that fit in your handbag. What's your opinion?"

"I don't have an opinion, ma'am. I never carry a handbag."

They reached the professor's garden. The rock was too large to have rolled under the fence, Andy noted, but it may have come through the gate if it had been open. In that case, what would have propelled it forward? Sure looks like she'd trespassed.

"Well?" demanded Tosca.

"Hmm. We'll be in touch. Thank you, ma'am."

"Aren't you going to go into the house and search around?"

"Not without a warrant. Goodbye, ma'am."

The two mounted their bicycles and rode away.

"No sense going any further with this," Andy told Bob. "We won't even need to file a report. She's off her rocker. What do you think?"

"I agree. It's just a damn big stone."

"My Dad's into this stuff," said Andy. "I'll give it to him."

"How's your Dad doing?"

"Gee, much better than I'd have thought. Since he retired from the Secret Service I've been after him to enjoy his hobby of geology more. Another good thing now that he's home, he and Christine have gotten closer. He still resists discussing her, though."

Andy went on to tell Bob that his father still occasionally took him camping to Joshua Tree National Park, the Mojave National Preserve and similar California desert areas to study rock formations and the wildlife.

"He mostly goes off alone, though, and when he comes back he tells me about the six-hundred-foot sand dunes, the magnificent granite peaks, the salt playas and the lost mines. But most of all, Dad loves rocks," Andy said, "any kind of rocks. His den at home is filled with dozens of them, all shapes, sizes and colors. So maybe this one from the loony lady will keep the old man occupied for a while. It sure is odd looking."

SEVEN

Thatch MacAulay stood uncertainly outside J.J.'s bright red Dutch door at the top of the wooden steps, shifting his six-foot, three-inch frame from one foot to another. When he'd called to ask if he could meet with her, Tosca had told him, "Oh, pop by any time."

In his left hand he held a paper bag containing the rock Andy had brought him and hoped against hope the old gal wasn't as gabby as his son reported. Thatch knew vaguely of Tosca Trevant's reputation as England's top gossip columnist. He'd heard about some kind of scandal she was recently involved in, but he'd paid no attention to the details.

Geology, on the other hand, topped his list of interests. He'd progressed from being a rock hound digging for semiprecious gems on outings with a local club to the serious study of geology, preferring to follow the pastime solo. Thatch found the pursuit of his hobby easy and rewarding, thanks to the rich variety of geological finds in the deserts, mountains, canyons and cliffs in the Southern and Central California regions.

Even though he had a pretty good idea of the composition of Tosca's rock, and his curiosity as to its origins was intense, he had a horror of loquacious little old ladies. However, he was as fascinated with the fossils themselves as with the rock that contained them, and he'd persuaded Andy, despite his reluctance, to play it by the book and open a case file at the police station. If the rock were to be tested at a state lab or at the FBI's forensics lab, it would need a file number to justify the lab time. His thoughts were suddenly interrupted when the door swung open.

"Oh, dear," said Tosca, glancing at MacAulay's Stetson. "Are you part of a posse?"

Thatch's eyebrows almost hit his hairline. He liked the way her sapphire blue eyes looked directly into his own and her expression of amusement and intelligence. Who was this? Not young enough to be the daughter, but certainly not the ancient crone he expected. As he eyed her blue tank top and white shorts, he watched her in return study him from head to toe. He was glad he'd polished his worn cowhide boots, no fancy ostrich or snakeskin for him, and wondered if she'd secretly flinched at his broken nose, suffered in his teens as a bronco rider on the college rodeo circuit.

"Mrs. Trevant?" He removed the rock from the bag.

"I am, indeed. Oh! You've brought it back."

He smiled broadly, hoping the calluses on his fingertips hadn't been too noticeable when they shook hands while the thought of his now-chunky physique caused him to suck in his stomach. He wasn't concerned about the deep furrows that radiated out from the edges of his eyes, nor the lines that cut across his forehead. His was a well-lived-in face midway into its fifth decade, and he made no excuses for it.

"I'm Andy's father. My son is the policeman you met a couple of days ago." He took off his hat. "And no, I'm not part of a posse, although our local sheriff can get one together when necessary." Which I know has never happened in swanky Newport Beach, he thought.

"Do come in." She led the way inside. "I'm just about to have a cup of tea. Would you join me? Please, sit down. My name is Tosca."

"Thank you. Please call me Thatch, short for Thatcher." At her raised eyebrows he quickly added, smiling, "No, nothing to do with your former prime minister, of course."

He set the rock on the coffee table and sat on the sofa, watching her fill an electric kettle with water at the kitchen sink.

"Uh, iced tea for me, if you don't mind."

Was she nuts? It was eighty-six degrees in today's unexpected spring heat wave.

"Iced?" said Tosca, turning to him and frowning.

No need for ice cubes, Thatch thought. Her chilly tone was enough to lower the temperature to thirty below.

"I'd be very grateful," she said, "if you would not mention iced tea in my presence. It's an abomination. Fancy making tea with beautifully boiled water which, by the way, must be poured over the leaves at the first puff of steam to avoid losing the oxygen, and then ruining it by adding ice."

"Well, then, maybe a soft drink?" he asked, watching her hips sway slightly as she walked toward the refrigerator. Talks a bit formal, but a beautiful woman. Son Andy needed a lecture or two.

"Here's something with tea in it that isn't hot, although it's said to warm the cockles of your heart," said Tosca. Instead of opening the refrigerator door, Tosca bent down beside it and picked up a small earthenware jug from the floor. "I think some mead would be far healthier than soda," she said, pouring an opaque, rust-colored liquid into a glass.

"Mead?" MacAulay chuckled. "That's some kind of English moonshine, right?"

"It's a natural honey wine. Some mead can taste more like beer. It's the beverage of the Vikings, the national drink of Ethiopia and of Mr. Pickwick, of course."

"Ethiopia?"

At his surprised expression she said, "Indeed. They call it *tej*. I brew my medieval Cornish mead using clover, heather or apple blossom honey plus sultanas, which are dried white grapes, malt extract and other ingredients. The rich color comes from adding half a cup of strong Darjeeling tea. I brought this batch with me. It's three years old. I think you'll find it most bracing."

Handing him the glass, she joined him on the sofa. He sipped the warm, cloying, sweet mixture. Man, must be thirty proof.

"Sure packs a punch," he admitted, feeling his taste buds instantly dive for cover. "Are you sure it's not moonshine, or is this more like dandelion wine?"

"Oh, no. Dandelion is one of the country wines, like parsnip, elderberry and nettle, but they all include pounds of refined sugar. Very bad for your teeth, although coltsfoot wine is wonderful for a cough. My *medh* is made with pure honey," she said, giving it its Gaelic pronunciation.

"Uh, maybe a few ice cubes?"

"One must drink *medh* at room temperature to appreciate its full body."

Thatch nodded his head in resignation.

"Now please tell me about this gruesome rock," said Tosca as Thatch took another small sip of the mead and replaced the glass on the coffee table.

"You could be right to be suspicious." He ran his fingers over the four small bony pieces that protruded. "I'm an amateur geologist. Really amateur, I'll admit, but I spend a lot of time on my hobby. Even so, this one has me beat. It sure looks like some of the round concretions I've studied in a couple of places in the California desert, but of course, I know darned well it isn't."

"Concretions? That's a new one to me. I assume they are some kind of rock. Is it common for them to have fossils embedded in them like these, if that's what they are?"

"As a matter of fact, yes, it is. Some are probably prehistoric. They form around a nucleus which can be a sea shell, a whale's tooth or most any other fossil like those right here. I've even seen a leaf in a limestone concretion."

"But why would these things be lined up like this as if they were four fingers?"

"Well, I have to agree with you," said Thatch. "It does look a little strange."

He frowned in concentration. Then he snapped his fingers. "Now I remember where I saw the rocks, in the desert near Ocotillo Wells, an off-road area south of here that's filled with sandstone concretions. It's called the Pumpkin Patch, but the globes are much larger than this one."

"I suppose they grow in your Pumpkin Patch," said Tosca, laughing.

"As a matter of fact they do. That's exactly what they do. They grow."

His serious demeanor cut short Tosca's merriment.

"Oh. Sorry," she said. "I didn't quite understand. I thought you meant they form over several centuries. When you mentioned pumpkins, however, I envisioned a short growing season."

"Geologists would have your head for that."

"Well, I'm sure you know your rock lore, but since you've never seen one with this exact formation, how can you be sure they aren't human fingertips or maybe someone's toes?"

It was Thatch's turn to laugh. "That is so unlikely, it's funny. Are you thinking of a caveman?"

He went on to describe concretions in greater detail, and she listened intently. "They're compacted, accumulated mineral matter that grows inside sedimentary rocks like shale and sandstone and even in volcanic rocks. They come in all shapes and sizes, round, square, long like a pipe, and can resemble a foot or a rib, though I must admit I've never come across a concretion like this."

When he stopped talking she told him of a criminal case in England involving fake rocks. A young man planned to kidnap a child and keep him as a sex slave. When he grew tired of the boy, she explained, the criminal planned to dismember him and chop the body into small pieces to create artificial rocks. Then he'd encase them in chicken wire before dipping them in cement. When they were dry the criminal was going to throw them into the sea off the coast of Scotland."

"And?" prompted Thatch.

"He was caught the day he kidnapped the boy, so fortunately he couldn't carry out his plan. He made a full confession, quite proud of his idea, so you can see my point about rocks."

"Yep, I do. Sure sounds like a sociopath."

"So what we shall we do next?" said Tosca.

Thatch was silent for a few moments, then said, "You know, I have a local FBI friend. I'll ask him if he can get this thing tested at the FBI lab at Quantico. They're usually really jammed up, but maybe there's a forensic anthropologist who'll be interested enough to do me a favor."

"Really? Excellent. How long will it take?"

"Couple of weeks, if I lean on him."

"Two weeks! The killer could be out there murdering more people!"

"Now don't jump the gun here. We don't know anything about a possible murder." Before she could voice a protest he added, "I'll see what I can do to hasten the result. Good day, ma'am, umm, Tosca."

Thatch stood up to leave. Wanting to kick himself for calling her ma'am, he retrieved his hat, put the rock back in the paper bag and left, promising to keep her informed of any developments. He got into his pickup, realizing he faced a dilemma. How am I going to convince my FBI buddies to give the test priority? As he considered the problem he also realized guiltily that in his absorption with Tosca he'd forgotten to check in with Christine. She'd be waiting impatiently for his call.

EIGHT

As soon as he finished talking to Christine, Thatch's cell phone rang again. Straining to hear, he pressed it tightly against his ear. Aging sucks, he thought, remembering his annual eye checkup when the doctor told him that it was normal for "our eyesight to degenerate as we age." He'd had to up the strength of his reading glasses to 250 from 175. Damn, is my hearing going, too?

"Andy, speak up, son. Repeat what you just said."

"Sorry, there's background noise here. Okay, I just wanted to check in with you about the weird rock and that eccentric woman on Isabel Island. I'm interested in what you think of her and her theory about a murder. Sounded like a real kook to me. My partner agrees."

"She's not a kook. I think there could be something to her story, and I'm going to help her check it out. Unofficially, of course."

"Really, Dad? Why? There wasn't much about her that caught my interest, unofficially or not." Andy's laugh sounded dismissive to Thatch, and he was quick to respond.

"You might be just as bad jumping to that conclusion, son, as Mrs. Trevant might be to hers. What's happened to your police training? If there is the possibility that a crime has been committed, if someone has been killed, there needs to be an investigation. There could be victims involved."

At Andy's silence Thatch continued, "There needs to be a passion from decent human beings to catch the perpetrator, to bring justice to bear. I know I sound like I'm lecturing you, but I thought you had that same sense of outrage as I do when I hear about teens shooting their parents, of little kids being kidnapped, raped and murdered. That's why you joined the police force, Andy, right? To respect law and order?"

"Dad, I thought you'd left all those emotions behind when you retired, and yeah, I did become a cop because of what you just said. But still, let's keep this in perspective. That woman's story sounds too far-fetched. It's Isabel Island, for God's sake. A music professor? Give me a break."

Thatch sighed audibly. "I'm not going to argue with you. We'll get back to that subject in ten years after you've got more experience under your belt and understand death and how the loss affects those left behind."

"Okay, okay, but there's no death here. What got me was the way she sounded so eager about the possibility of there being real fingers inside that rock. That's pretty heartless, isn't it?"

Thatch thought back to the most serious of the presidential assassination attempts he'd been involved in as a Secret Service officer and having to shoot to kill and how he'd felt about it afterward. Was he, too, heartless? There was never time to evaluate emotions when various incidents occurred, but the stress had built up through the years. When circumstances in his personal life changed, and retirement wasn't far off, he was more than ready to quit the Service. Besides, now he had more time for Christine.

He spoke into the phone again. "Andy, maybe that's Mrs. Trevant's way of dealing with something that's too horrible for her to think about. On the other hand, don't forget that she's a journalist. She knows all about grim realities."

"Sure, Dad. Covering Buckingham Palace?" Andy's chuckle echoed in Thatch's ear.

"Look, son," he said, "right now I want you to treat this thing seriously. Did you open a case file like I asked?

You probably don't have a lot of currently active cases, do you?"

"Just the usual stuff. Our file jackets right now are mostly domestic violence, drunk driving, petty theft, a couple of hit-and-runs, missing persons and graffiti. And yes, I opened a file on the incident with Mrs. Trevant at your insistence, but I felt like an idiot about it. You know, I could have charged her with trespassing."

"I'll be sure to tell her that when I see her again."

"So, Dad, did you come to some conclusion about the rock?"

"Yep."

"And?"

"Well, son, I've got some ideas I'm batting around. Nothing I want to share right now, though." Changing the subject, he said, "Life still good?"

"Yeah. I met a girl."

"And?"

"Nothing I want to share right now."

Thatch laughed. "Point taken. 'Bye, kid. Keep those bicycle tires pumped."

NINE

Professor Whittaker was on Tosca's mind all morning. What had his wife been like? Was there really a crime here she could solve? Wouldn't hurt to nose around. She decided to pay a call on Arlene Mindel, who lived across the street. She and Tosca had become friendly after discovering they both shared an interest in gossip.

"Hello, there," said Tosca after Arlene opened the door. "I wonder if you would like to come over to our flat for a cup of tea or a glass of mead?" At Arlene's shudder Tosca inquired if she was coming down with a cold.

"No, I'm fine, and thanks, but, umm, I need to stay close to the phone. Come on in and have some coffee with me."

Arlene was one of the original residents of Isabel Island, and Tosca enjoyed listening to her stories. A squirrel of a woman, she constantly darted here and there about her kitchen, refilling Tosca's coffee cup before she'd barely taken a sip or moving like lightning to mop up a milk spill. Her short, brown, stick-straight hair and pear-shaped figure were a familiar sight on the island, and with a warm, motherly personality, she was popular among her neighbors. Arlene had told Tosca she retired from her job as an accountant ten years earlier, inheriting the beach house from her parents, who were among the first to settle there when it was barely more than a man-made sandbar, and primitive beach shacks were the order of the day.

Tosca hoisted herself up onto one of the tall barstools at Arlene's kitchen counter, trying unsuccessfully to find a more comfortable perch for her feet. She could barely reach the rungs with her toes. Why can't Americans sit in proper chairs, she thought as Arlene poured more coffee. Stools and bar counters seem to be a national compulsion, and installing granite counter tops is an absolute mania. Still, Americans are much more hospitable and generous than Brits, she reflected, and their coffee is terrific.

"How's J.J.? Still racing?"

"Yes, indeed. She won last week. Arlene, I wanted to ask you about the professor up the street. I'm kind of curious about him."

"Ah. You know, Tosca, he's only been a widower for a short time. Isn't it a little soon to expect him to start dating?"

"Oh, that's funny. Please, it's nothing like that. I'm not the least bit interested in him romantically. Heaven forbid. No, I just admire his music. I wondered if you knew him when he and his wife first came to live here."

"Sure, we met the day they moved in. They had to take out that huge front window to get the piano inside. It caused a real commotion, and I was outside watching. Marcia and Jerry Steiner, the previous owners, would've had a fit if they'd seen it. The professor is never friendly, though. Very aloof, not like Monica, God grant her peace."

"What was she like?" asked Tosca.

"Meticulous around the house, from the few times I was there," replied Arlene. "She loved shopping, wore wonderful clothes. 'Course, she had a terrific figure. But she told me she always had to nag the professor for an allowance. She was kind of flighty. Not much in her head aside from tennis. But he was crazy about her, at least at first. Indulgent as all get out. She could wrap him around her little finger, but then I guess the novelty wore off."

"How do you mean?"

"Maybe it was because of his marrying for the first time so late in life and she being a lot younger. They'd have arguments. You could hear it clear down to the end of the street."

"He seems so mild. What did they argue about?"

"Sure, he's mild, all right. She was the one that did all the screaming. She'd shout him into silence." Arlene's voice lowered to a whisper. "I once heard Monica call her husband impotent, but that was years ago. Their rows were mostly on account of her flirting with everyone she met. She was incorrigible. He used to have music students come to the house for lessons, but Monica got too friendly. She'd be joshing with them even before they got inside. You could see it from here. Monica laughed about it when I said something. She told me Haiden finally rented a studio. Only one of his young students came to the house after that, and he was absolutely brilliant. We'd hear that piano sing like an angel."

"I'm surprised someone like Monica would marry an older man like that, especially one so obese."

"He used to be skinny, and he was famous locally. She liked that. Then, too, there was the cachet of living in Newport Beach and belonging to the Barracuda Bay Club. I think she came from somewhere inland, nowhere fancy. But after they'd been married a year or so, Haiden began to put on weight, and the rows started. Now, he's as big as a house."

"I don't get the connection," said Tosca.

"It was sweet, when you think about it. He did all the cooking, he really got into it. Wish I could say the same for my husband. The professor went out and bought the best kitchen equipment and gadgets he could find and even asked my opinion of food processors. When his cousin and her husband came down from Northern California, Monica invited us over, and Haiden cooked the whole meal."

"Why did he do all the cooking?"

Arlene shrugged. "Monica wasn't the domestic type. Maybe he liked fixing romantic dinners."

"The professor is a premier composer, I hear," said Tosca.

"Not any more. My brother-in-law told me his last piano concerto was an awful embarrassment."

Tosca wondered how the professor handled the humiliation. Then she took another tack.

"So the professor has a cousin?"

"Yes," said Arlene. "Betty Garrison and her husband, Frank, are both dentists at their clinic in San Francisco, but I only saw them here that one time about three years ago. They were attending a dental convention in Newport Beach, so naturally they spent a few days with the Whittakers on the island."

"Did you spend any time with the Garrisons?"

"No. Monica had us over to the house once for cocktails, and there was the dinner, of course, and one day when Frank went off to join a deep-sea fishing party, I took Betty to the Barracuda Bay Club for a fashion show. I should take you to our next one."

Not my cup of tea, thought Tosca. "Thanks, but I am often working. I'm a reporter, you know."

"Yes, I heard you were some kind of writer."

Arlene suddenly scampered over to the oven and pulled down the door. The aroma of baking cookies filled the kitchen. She peered at them as closely as a squirrel would inspect a prize cache of acorns, nodded once and closed the door. Returning to her coffee, she said, "You're a gossip columnist, I think J.J. told me. Well, there's plenty of gossip here on the island."

"Actually, I'm working on a criminal case right now."

Arlene's head bobbed up. "Criminal case? Here?" She laughed. "Oh, you mean one of those white collar frauds, a Ponzi scheme?"

"No, but I can't discuss it. Confidential, you know. It could involve some bones. And yes, here on the island."

"My goodness! Well, you know what? Talking of bones reminds me of something that Betty told me, something really weird and to my mind cruel, if not criminal."

"Oh?"

"We were talking about where we went to school and where we were raised. I was telling her how great it was that my parents lived at the beach. She said she lived on a ranch, and the Whittaker family spent summers there for a few years. I asked Betty about the professor's talent, if it was evident as a young boy. She said they all recognized his gift when he was five years old."

"Five! As young as that?"

"Yes. Betty said that most of the time there he sat for hours at the piano. But one summer her dad discovered Haiden had mutilated a dead rabbit, chopped off its paws and stuck them inside his Play-Doh. Said they were ornaments. After that, Betty told me, Haiden wasn't allowed to visit any more." Arlene shivered. "Imagine, he was just a child!"

"Takes all kinds, if you'll forgive the cliché," said Tosca. "Uh, Arlene, I think the cookies are burning."

Arlene opened the oven. A cloud of gray smoke poured out. She shrugged, slid the burnt cookies onto a plate and put the cookie sheet in the sink, ignoring the smell.

"Happens all the time," she said. "I really should set the timer."

Tosca gestured toward Arlene's garden outside the front window. "I've been admiring your delphiniums. I'm amazed at the many flowers you can grow here, especially during the winter. What was the previous owners' garden like, before Haiden bought the house?" She slid off the barstool, unable to bear its discomfort.

"Hmm, well, they had a couple of pink and white oleander bushes in the front. Marcia loved those, but they got some kind of disease and died. Maybe it was a bug."

"How about that corner area that's built up into a rock garden? She must have been loath to leave it."

"Oh, no. The Steiners didn't put that there. Aside from the oleanders Marcia wasn't much for gardening. Jerry, though, he was handy with tools. He liked to do woodwork. After he died and the house was sold to the professor, I was surprised that she left all of her husband's tools in the garage. He was always sharpening some blade or another. As for the rock garden, Haiden built it himself. We all admired its beauty. It was unusual to see one like that because our yards are so small, but he did a very nice job. The last couple of years he's neglected it, though."

Well, well, thought Tosca. He lied to me. Good. I just knew something was fishy. She thanked her neighbor for the coffee, said goodbye and returned home. In her bedroom she searched through the several dozen music CDs she'd brought from England and picked out Virgil Thomson's "Four Saints in Three Acts." She disliked the opera's religious music but had great respect for Gertrude Stein's surreal libretto.

Leaving the house again, she walked over to the professor's home and rang the doorbell. She knew he was there because the leather chair was occupied. As usual, his head was buried in the newspaper, a half-eaten sandwich on a side table nearby. A late lunch, observed Tosca.

After a few moments the front door opened. "Ah! Haiden! I've brought you a CD. The music is quite uncommon, and I thought it would be charming to listen to it together."

"Menotti's 'The Telephone?'" he asked sarcastically.

"Bravo," she said. "You know that little comic opera. No, no, this is a decade or so older. Umm, may I come in?"

"I'm about to go out."

"Quite all right. I'll come back later."

Aiming somewhere at his expansive middle, Tosca thrust the CD at him, and he instinctively raised a hand to grasp it. She walked quickly away. At the gate Tosca turned to give him a sweet smile, but the professor had already closed the door.

TEN

Whittaker unfolded his stocky frame from the piano bench and ambled to the den, a room at the rear of the house, the refuge that had served him so well during his marriage to Monica. Ah, Monica.

Funny how the time between the two deaths seemed so short. Those intervening five years had not been happy for him, although they seemed to have been for her, he reflected. Their relationship deteriorated rapidly after what happened to Paul Holloway, his favorite student. He never forgave her for that, although they didn't speak of it again until those final moments when he took his revenge. Sure, he knew of her infidelities, and he'd caught her many times, eyeing his students when they came to study with him at home, but after Paul she was very careful not to linger.

"What time is your next student arriving?" she'd ask every Tuesday and Thursday evening.

"Don't be tiresome, Monica. You know very well that they always arrive on the hour or a few minutes before," he'd say, his answer always the same.

"I'll stay out of your way then. I'll be at the club courts," she'd answer, flouncing off dressed in her latest designer tennis outfit. It was an exchange they had each week, and he'd grown tired of the charade. He didn't even bother to comment when she frequently left her favorite tennis racket behind. Eventually, he rented a small studio for the classes. Only Paul continued to come to the house for lessons.

Since that terrible night it was inevitable, he supposed, that he and Monica would change, he with his creativity stifled and Monica out partying with friends later than ever.

He'd been unable to produce even the semblance of a new composition despite sitting at the piano week after week, month after month. For several years he'd happily composed music for dance and theater productions at the university, appreciating how it advanced his career; but lately he'd failed miserably. Each piece he offered was received in silence and remained unused. It was her fault, of course,

Monica was almost out of control, he saw. She drank constantly, her youthful looks gaining a harshness. She lost weight, and the thinness of her face emphasized encroaching wrinkles. When she wasn't around for meals, he'd taken to grilling a steak and microwaving frozen fries, or else he brought home fast food. Then there were the social and fundraising dinners to which he was occasionally invited. The result was all too obvious, he thought, patting his bulging belly. Quite the opposite outcome to his wife's, he chuckled.

He never should have married her in the first place. It was a freak incident. She had caught him at a vulnerable time when he was lionized locally and in ever-widening artistic circles for his talent. His music scores were selling well, and he was a guest pianist at many of the most prestigious concert venues. The success went to his head, he admitted now, and he was ripe for plucking. When he first met Monica at the Barracuda Bay Club where he was accepting yet another award, he felt like a conqueror. People were fawning over him, as usual, wanting to talk or listen, martinis in hand. He sensed he could have his pick of the women there, at least the older ones and maybe one or two of the married ones. Then he'd heard a soft, girlish voice whispering in his ear.

"Professor Whittaker, you truly are a genius. May I speak to you for a moment?"

She'd sidled up to his table where he was sitting with some of his colleagues from UCI. He figured she had her eye on John, opposite him, or Bill at his left; but as she continued to focus her entire attention on him Whittaker realized this buxom young blonde in the blue dress and diamond necklace really did want to talk to him.

"Of course. I'm afraid there are no empty seats," the professor said, turning to her and rising from his chair, "but perhaps we could talk afterwards."

She'd given him a flirty glance, shaken her curls and said, "I'll make sure I'm waiting for you. In the bar."

She'd been cunning, he granted her that. Obviously knowing his reputation, she began by asking about his latest composition. As it happened, he had just completed one that very afternoon, an hour before the banquet, so he was delighted to talk to her about it, saying she was the first person to hear its title. Monica claimed she'd sung in light opera, performing most often in *Yeoman of the Guard*.

She and the professor launched into a spirited discussion, albeit one-way, of the state of the current crop of classical compositions with him doing all the talking, he recalled. He asked if she'd like to hear some of his own music at his home.

The romance progressed rapidly. He grimaced at the remembrance, especially after she visited his bay front house and saw his neighbors' yachts tied up at their private docks. Before he knew it, he'd proposed. Her true taste in music, he soon learned, was hard rock, although he once found her listening to Shostakovich's "Song of the Forest," which he conceded was classical but still as gaudy as the Las Vegas wedding chapel where she'd insisted they exchange vows. He discovered, too, that she was no daughter of wealthy parents who lived in Portugal, as she claimed, but had been brought up in a foster family. When the flirtations and arguments began, he asked her why she married him. After all, she was only twenty-five at the time. Surely many men had sought her out.

"They were smarter than you," she replied, her candor shocking him. "I made the right moves, but the rich guys I met took the trouble to check me out." She readily admitted her delight that it never occurred to the professor, his head in the clouds, to do the same. Suddenly he was a married man.

Now, as he recalled Tosca's visit and their conversation about the rock garden, Whittaker picked up his cell phone and dialed.

"I'm ready to sell the collection."

He hung up and went into the den. Three of its walls were lined with shelves, overflowing with musical scores, librettos, arrangements, books, CDs and tapes, like the living room. The east wall was dominated by an oil painting. Opposite, a large, freestanding vault occupied an alcove. It had been installed at Monica's suggestion, although the jewelry she kept in it was worthless, he always thought.

After his wife left for a week to visit her Aunt Ginny in Denver, Whittaker arranged for his own small safe to be built into the east wall, hidden behind DelRossi's spectacular "Cameo Cascade." Painted in the early 1900s, it glowed with the rosy light of a river of sparkling cameo-pink diamonds tumbling over a gorge, sunlight striking every facet, sending up a shower of stars. Whittaker appreciated its significance, but diamonds weren't his passion. What started out as a teenage hobby after a neighbor gave him some World War II Japanese coins had grown into a secret obsession over the years, providing the perfect counterpoint to his music.

Swinging the painting to one side on its hinges, he opened the safe and removed four long steel trays. He placed them on his desk and gently unwrapped the velvet pouches they held. Inside the pouches were one hundred two-inch by two-inch cellophane envelopes, protection for the gold, silver and copper coins they contained.

Stapled to each envelope was a small index card with the date, condition and identification of each piece.

"Come along, my beauties," he murmured. "It's time to find you a new home. Monica was going to turn you over to the police after discovering your hiding place. What a tragedy that would have been."

Whittaker knew it wouldn't be easy to locate a collector willing to buy these pieces at short notice, because several had been stolen from the world's top museums. It had taken Whittaker more than two decades to accumulate the treasures, negotiating through second, third and fourth parties, a few of them thieves, most greedy businessmen, others desperate for cash.

Many of the museums didn't even know some of their treasures were missing. With cavernous cellars and warehouses filled with containers from donated collections, as well as discoveries by archeologists and exhibits on loan, the museums and galleries had hundreds of items in storage.

Several years earlier Whittaker had recruited a handful of his foreign music students to apply for research credentials at the British Museum, the Cairo Art Gallery and other conservatories that allowed academics access to their storerooms. It was common knowledge in the antiquities market that a surprising number of curators kept poor inventories. It was easy for Whittaker to pay students to pocket small items like ancient coins that had not yet been sorted and catalogued.

He'd received a portion of his illegal collection from the State Hermitage Museum in St. Petersburg, Russia. The four Unicorn gold coins of Scotland, dated 1486, were from the Australian Museum where a "steal-to-order" scandal was later uncovered. Whittaker had lost count of the number of museums that, in fact, had been pillaged on his behalf.

The professor paused for a moment, his eyes fixed on rows of Egyptian scepters, English ducats, Persian darics, silver pennies, Greek drachmas and two dozen of America's first minted coins. Did he really need to sell? The house might fetch two million, the pension would cover normal living expenses, and the royalties from his music, though not high, should add yet another financial cushion. So why not keep the coins? As he opened one of the envelopes, he recalled an earlier conversation.

"Never touch the coins with your bare hands," an expert had told him.

"Why not? I like their resistance, their hardness, so different from piano keys that give in to the slightest pressure."

The expert smiled at him condescendingly. "Fingerprints and body oil can mar the surface of a coin for years. Even a tiny drop of moisture can cause oxidation. Keep your coins in an air-tight safe with the humidity level at thirty-eight percent."

Trained in a lifetime of discipline as a musician, Whittaker thereafter never once gave in to his desire to hold the coins without their protective envelopes. Instead, forced to admire his treasure through their protective covering, he soon realized that the expert's admonition added an exciting new dimension to his attitude toward the collection. It made his hoard more sacred and pure. He could worship it as an untouchable icon, yet know it was as tempting as forbidden fruit.

It was a trait Whittaker had carried over into other areas of his life, including Monica, at least for the first year or two of their marriage. Surprised at himself for being wed to a much younger woman, even bemused that he'd actually taken a bride, he had initially treated her with kid gloves, almost afraid to caress the silky, white skin.

He remembered a couple of previous romantic encounters, both in college. One coed he dated was a pharmacy student, but his obsessive music practice, hour after hour, drove her away. The other was an athlete who came to despise his disdain of sports. Even fellow female musicians failed to be attracted to him, which Whittaker attributed to his attitude, considered by his peers to be one of veiled arrogance. Later, his professorship at UCI, where he was esteemed, and growing fame led to invitations to events and parties where his reputation gained him attention; but one by one the women he dated as a result soon dropped him.

Whittaker realized he hadn't added to his coin collection in two years, certainly not since Monica's real estate company had gone bust. Obviously, his desire and obsession had dimmed. All right, time to start fresh. That meant the coins must go. In a hurry to leave, he transferred the velvet pouches into a small calfskin leather attaché case, closed the locks and returned the empty trays to the wall safe. Then he closed the safe and swung the painting back into place.

He checked his watch. Damn. He'd almost forgotten. There were still four more hours to wait. Although they'd had no contact for six years, he guessed that coin broker Gustave Vernays still permitted no one to visit him before nine p.m. When Whittaker had purchased a rare 1619 hammered gold laurel coin and a Roman denarius, equally as rare and considered a masterpiece of numismatic art, he'd arrived fifteen minutes early and been forced to cool his heels outside the door.

Now, too unsettled to sit still, the professor spent the time packing the rest of Monica's belongings into boxes for donation to Goodwill. The thought of this generous gesture was the most gratifying he'd felt in a long time.

Finally the grandfather clock chimed eight-thirty. Clutching the attaché case, Whittaker was about to close the door behind him when something compelled him to look back. His glance went straight to the shiny, dime-sized circle on the dark blue carpet under the DelRossi painting. The coin must have slipped out of its envelope. In three strides, he bent to pick up the silver Greek aegina by its edges, but then, in a fit of perversity, deliberately pressed the coin between fingers and thumb and closed his fist around it. What did it matter if he soiled its surface now? He dropped the coin into his jacket pocket.

In the garage the professor eased into his car and placed the coin collection on the passenger seat. He switched on the Jaguar's ignition and backed out, heading for Center Street. He drove across the bridge and headed up Jamboree Boulevard, past the exclusive Big Canyon Country Club and several gated estates, toward the Santa Ana freeway. Around him, Rolls-Royces, Mercedes-Benzes, BMWs, Range Rovers and Ferraris cruised the streets. But when he left behind Newport's pristine, landscaped borders, the upscale cars gave way to Chevrolets, Fords and Suzuki pickup trucks.

He drove by the local airport. Located a few miles north of Newport Beach's stretch of shore, it had been transformed a decade earlier from a mown field with a few short runways and small buildings into a bustling terminal. Whittaker often flew out of there but disliked the fact that the growth was in response to the real estate development of Orange County. He resented the way it gobbled up farmland and ranches, spawning financial institutions and banks to create a mini-Wall Street on Newport Center Drive.

"We're in a fabulous boom," Monica had assured him at the time. "We're going to be multi-millionaires!" Her small partnership in a real estate company funded by Whittaker found her among leading developers as they feverishly bought up strawberry fields, orange groves and cattle pastures, building thousands of condominiums and cluster homes in their place. The structures crept up every ridge and overlooked each canyon, the relentless march of a silent army of dwellings whose uniforms were white stucco and whose helmets were red Spanish tile.

Everyone wanted everything, thought Whittaker as he waited impatiently for a traffic light to turn green. In Newport Beach that translated into sleek cars, sleek women and sleek boats. Later came the real estate crash. Monica's company had folded, and she'd lost her shirt. He smiled at the memory. She'd sulked for days. Although he'd put up the money, he could afford the loss, which was less interesting to him than his wife's failure.

ELEVEN

Whittaker arrived at Vernays' high-rise condominium building, parked in the private underground garage after punching in the access code and made his way to the coin dealer's penthouse. He rang the bell, turning to wave a greeting to the security camera mounted on the ceiling. Vernays opened the door and ushered the professor inside.

"Sit down, sit down," he said, indicating the ornate Louis XV sofa.

"I won't be here long enough." Whittaker removed the velvet bundles from his attaché case and handed them to Vernays, who laid them on the coffee table and unfolded them to reveal the coins. "Sell them, Gustave. All of them. Must be worth five million by now."

Vernays' narrow lips pursed. Thin as a steeple, his lean, lined face was marred by large, puffy bags under pale blue eyes. His short, blond hair had turned completely white, Whittaker realized, since he'd had last seen him.

"What's wrong?" said the professor. "No buyers? Surely the market hasn't dried up."

"It will take a while," the Swiss murmured, his veined hands stroking the edges of the velvet covers as he bent closer to the collection spread before him. "What a wealth of world history these coins represent. Most impressive but," his tone became brisk as he straightened up, "there will be a problem regarding their actual value."

Whittaker felt his body tense. "Why? They're in superb condition, Gustave. Besides, you already know their value. I bought many of these pieces through you. I know very well that rare coins are the most liquid of all collectibles."

"I have to make sure each one is genuine," Vernays said.

"Now wait a minute. If there are any fakes here, they're on your head. Each of the coins I acquired on my own has an impeccable provenance. I know their exact origins."

"Calm yourself, Haiden. Let's go into my study. "Vernays carefully gathered up the velvet covers. He led the way to the back of his apartment, to a windowless room insulated with concrete walls covered top to bottom with rare fifteenth century tapestries. Here, in complete privacy, he and his sellers and buyers were able to barter over coins that originated from all four corners of the world. Vernays dealt only with multimillionaire private collectors and insisted on conducting business in person at his home in the sealed room. He was also known never to raise his voice or deceive a client despite striking a hard bargain. Cheating the authorities was something else again.

The furnishings in the room were as luxurious as the medieval Belgian tapestries. A large French Renaissance sofa and two wingback chairs filled the space. Vernays sat down behind the ornate, gilt-trimmed desk, indicating a chair to the professor. Whittaker remained standing.

"Please, sit down. I've never seen you so upset," Vernays said. "Why so aggressive?"

"I'm in no mood to be cheated."

"Don't insult me." Vernays' voice was sharp. "We've done business for years. I don't appreciate your attitude. Leave the collection with me, and I'll start working on it."

The coin dealer got up abruptly and walked to the door, expecting his visitor to follow. When Whittaker remained standing in front of his coins, Vernays raised his eyebrows.

"Surely you don't want a receipt, Haiden. You know how careful I am about leaving a paper trail."

"It isn't that. I'm not sure now whether I want to sell the entire collection. Maybe I'll keep these." He picked out five cellophane envelopes, two containing gold coins. The three other envelopes held silver coins. He put them inside his attaché case. "All right. Find me a buyer for the rest," he said.

Vernays walked him to the door, and the professor left with no further comment. Within minutes he had descended in the elevator and found his car in the parking structure.

By now it was ten o'clock. Whittaker realized he hadn't eaten dinner and decided to go to his favorite Thai restaurant across the bay. He drove south to Isabel Island and reached the seafront. After parking the Jaguar on a side street he boarded the ferry and sat on one of the wooden side benches, watching the water traffic, sparse at this hour.

"That's a dollar, sir."

Whittaker pulled his gaze away from the string of lights that silhouetted the roof of the Pavilion restaurant on the opposite side of the bay, reached into his trouser pocket and found some loose change.

"Here," he said. He picked out three quarters, a dime and a nickel, leaving three pennies that he returned to his pocket. "Used to be twenty cents a few years back," he said, sizing up the skinny youth whose name tag read Todd. Working on the ferries was a coveted evening job for local university students after classes. The ferry company hired two people for each boat, one to operate it and one to collect fares. Monica's nephew had spent a couple of summers working on them.

"I know, sir, but the fare went up again Monday, and you've only given me ninety cents."

The professor patted his jacket pockets, still looking at the student who reminded him of himself at that age, living on scholarships, working two jobs, hustling patrons at the local piano bar and eager for life.

"Ah. Here. Another dime."

"Thanks, that'll do it, sir."

After the ferry docked, Whittaker walked two blocks to the restaurant, a small hideaway favored by locals. At this late hour it was empty, but he was pleased to find himself welcomed.

"Good evening, Professor." The slender Thai woman bowed gracefully from the waist. "We read your wife's obituary in the newspaper. Please accept our deep sympathy."

"Thank you, Lampai. Very much appreciated."

"Your usual order? The chef is ready to go home."

"Anything you can serve me is fine."

After a four-course meal of coconut soup with mushrooms, shrimp in sweet chili sauce, pineapple fried rice and garlic chicken, the professor ordered a third Singha beer before asking for his check. Life was wonderful. As he waited to pay he glanced at the soft, sea green Asian celadon chinaware and the lotus-shaped candleholders on the other tables. He admired, as usual, the walls covered in brilliant blue and crimson Thai silk.

Draining the last drops of beer from his glass, head tilted back, his eyes lit on the familiar, small gold Buddha statue enshrined high on a shelf almost at ceiling level, trails of incense smoke spiraling lazily from a small brass pot next to it. Tonight the candles on each side of the statue burned brightly, throwing the Buddha's laughing yellow face into sharp relief against the wall, reminding him of the grinning god on the face of one of his Greek fourth century B.C. coins.

Whittaker's pleasure abruptly ended. Panicked, he stood up and thrust his hands into both jacket pockets, pressing his fingers deep into the empty corners. He pulled his trouser pockets inside out. Nothing. He had definitely slipped the silver coin he'd dropped on the floor at home into his jacket pocket before visiting Vernays. Anxiety and fear flashed through his body when he realized what had happened.

TWELVE

The last ferry left at midnight, and Whittaker had to hustle his considerable bulk to catch it. He was the sole passenger. Newport Beach rolled up its sidewalks early in the off-season, and the harbor was deserted. No other boat traffic was in sight as the pilot steered across the channel. Within minutes he was pulling into the dock and snapping the ferry's wide metal bar onto two stanchions to secure it. The pilot said a quick goodnight to the fare collector and hurried off.

"Fog rolling in, sir," Todd said to Whittaker as they debarked onto the dock.

"Do you remember me from earlier this evening, Todd? I gave you three quarters, a nickel and two dimes. One of the dimes was, well, kind of new. I saw you looking at it. Maybe you kept it for yourself. It was very shiny. Anyway, I need it back, kid. Now."

"Jeez, I've collected a lot of coins since then. What was so special about it?"

"Oh, nothing, nothing. Sentimental value, that's all."

Whittaker watched Todd's eyes narrow.

"Exactly how much value?"

"Nothing. It's just a dime, that's all."

Stupid kid, thought Whittaker. How dare he threaten me with extortion. Damned if I'm going to pay through the nose to get it back. "Look, here's five bucks. Now give me the coin."

"I don't have it on me. The bag of fares I took in earlier when you were here is locked up." He waved a hand toward the small wooden building near the dock that served as an office. "I have to total my takings. I need time to do that at the end of the day. If I find the coin, I'll keep

73

it for you. You could come back in half an hour. Maybe you can figure out what it's really worth to you by then."

Todd smirked, turned his back on the professor and sauntered off toward the office. Before entering, the youth turned around and shouted, "Hey, you! Old man! Fatty! When you come back, bring plenty of money!"

As the door closed behind Todd Whittaker felt the familiar flash of hot rage sweep through him. Arrogant, insulting kid. With the words still ringing in his ears, Whittaker's anger increased. First that Tosca woman and now this.

After his head cleared and his emotions were under control, the professor left the seafront and hurried down Parker Street, passing the covered florist stand and the trendy ceramic gallery. He didn't stop until he'd turned the corner and found his car. Whittaker drove home and, once inside the garage, sat to think for a few minutes. It's my aegina. It's mine! That ignorant kid is treating this like some scumbag blackmail affair. It's probably in the boy's dirty hand and being dropped into a filthy jeans pocket, he thought.

Sure, plenty of other coins in his collection were worth much more, but Todd's attempt to make a few bucks off the aegina stuck in the professor's craw.

With a grunt, he exited the Jaguar and went to the back of the car. He opened the trunk, removed the tire iron and slammed the trunk lid closed. He threw the tire iron onto the passenger seat, got back into the driver's side and drove out of the garage, parking once more within three blocks of the ferry office.

"It's mine," he repeated as he got out of the car, "and if he's not there, if he's left, I'll just break in and get it unless he's taken it with him."

Before leaving the car door slightly ajar in case he had to beat a hasty retreat, the professor switched off the vehicle's roof light and made his way to the ferry office as quickly and softly as his corpulence would allow.

Bands of pale light shone through the broken strips of venetian blinds that covered the windows at the back of the shack. Whittaker could see the boy inside counting money into a brown bank deposit bag. A few minutes later the light was extinguished. Todd opened the office door, wheeling a bicycle. Tied with a bungee cord to the rear bike carrier was the bank bag. Seeing the professor, he stopped just outside the door frame and said, "Hey, I've got your coin here. It's not a dime, you know? Looks old. Must be worth a few hundred, right?"

Whittaker approached Todd and swung the tire iron. The weapon cracked against the boy's head. He crumpled to the ground, hitting the concrete boardwalk. The bicycle fell back into the office, the bank bag escaping its tether and bursting open. Hundreds of nickels, dimes, quarters, and dollar bills spewed onto the floor, the coins rolling in all directions.

Todd moaned as a pool of blood stained the sidewalk. Setting the tire iron aside Whittaker knelt down and, ignoring the blood that began to soak into the edges of his jacket sleeves, grabbed the boy's neck with both hands. The professor squeezed for several moments before releasing him. He checked the boy's pulse and breathing once more. Nothing. Where's my aegina? In the bank bag? No, it wouldn't have been mixed it in with all those nickels, dimes and quarters. He'd already looked through the boy's pockets. Empty. Had the kid been holding it in those grimy hands? He pried open Todd's fingers and found a 2002 U.S. dime clenched in his right palm. Looks like the stupid kid figured he could fool me with it, take the blackmail money and sell the Greek coin himself. So where is it?

It took several attempts before Whittaker was able to stand up from his kneeling position. Suddenly feeling vulnerable, he looked around. The boardwalk remained deserted, but the distant sound of a car starting up startled him. He knew he had to hide the body. There was no way he could back up his car close enough to the boardwalk to load the body into the trunk, and Todd was too heavy to carry three blocks to the Jaguar. Whittaker saw a small, covered, flat-bottomed rowboat a few yards away, pulled up onto the sand. He knew that owners often left their boats there for days. He dragged the corpse to the boat and left it on the sand while he pushed aside the canvas cover. The professor heaved the corpse up and into the boat and pulled the cover back in place.

The struggle winded him, and he had to rest his bulk against the side of the boat for a few moments. As he did so he noticed a few drops of blood had dripped onto the sand. He saw a pile of seaweed nearby, bent down to pick it up and laid it over the blood. When he straightened up he saw that although the body had fallen onto its back across the boat's bench seats and was now hidden under the canvas, one of the youth's legs was hanging over the side and in full sight, its knee bent and the foot almost touching the sand. Whittaker grabbed the errant leg to push it back under the canvas but paused as he heard the familiar muted droning of a Sheriff's Department harbor patrol boat pierce the quiet of the night.

"Damn!" He ducked down again. Often while composing he would look up from his piano to watch the vessel's slow progress around the bay as it monitored boat traffic. A few years earlier it had accidentally run over and killed Newport Harbor's resident black swan, causing quite a controversy, but no one protested enough to have the night patrols cut back.

After the craft cruised by the professor once again tried to push the dangling foot under the rowboat's cover, failed, and knew he had to leave before the patrol boat reached the other end of the bay and turned around.

Whittaker went back to his car. The Jaguar's clock read 3:14 a.m. He sat inside and waited fifteen minutes before getting out again, allowing the patrol boat time to glide slowly by on its way to make the rounds of the other six islands in the bay. When it was well out of sight Whittaker returned to the ferry office for a more thorough search.

He found the light switch and began looking around the small room. It contained a battered desk, a metal folding chair, a three-tiered file cabinet and a shelf that held four coffee mugs alongside a coffee pot and a can of coffee. Where would a kid hide a coin? Coffee can? Not there. Coffee cups? Sugar bin? Under the tattered grasscloth rug? Against the far wall stood a sturdy steel safe. There was little worth stealing, he saw, and assumed that the safe held only each day's takings, which were later emptied into the bag and set inside a bank night deposit box. Whittaker inspected the small toilet and opened a second door to a broom closet. The walls were bare of shelves, and linoleum covered the floor. So, he thought, the coin is not in the closet or bathroom or above the door sill. Surely it had to be with the boy, because he'd told Whittaker to come back later with blackmail money.

After half an hour he had to admit the aegina was not in the office as far as he could determine. Neither was it on the kid. Whittaker had searched the boy's clothes thoroughly. It certainly wouldn't have been mixed in among those hundreds of other coins in the bank bag. His rage and frustration mounting, he told himself that the kid may have have passed it on to a friend for safekeeping or mistakenly given it to a passenger as change, as he himself had.

He checked his watch. The patrol boat would be in sight again soon. Before leaving the ferry office he found a hand towel in the small bathroom, grabbed it and wiped the surfaces of everything he'd touched including the broom, the dustpan and the bicycle. Taking one final look around, he used the towel on the door handle when he closed it and took the towel with him, along with the tire iron.

Only in the morning did he remember that he hadn't returned to the small boat to hide the boy's leg.

THIRTEEN

Homicide Detective Wally Parnell and two other officers from the Major Crime Scene Unit showed up at the ferry office at six thirty-six a.m. The first uniforms to arrive, fifteen minutes earlier, had already strung yellow tape around the area, cutting off access from both sides of the seafront walkway. The ferries were ordered to stop running until the crime scene was cleared.

On the beach the rowboat was being inspected by forensics, dusted for prints, and photographed. Measurements had been taken. A preliminary sketch of the scene was made; when the officer got back to the station he'd make a more detailed drawing.

A police helicopter droned overhead and a television news chopper circled the area. Two reporters stood at the yellow tape line among a small group of onlookers, waiting for Parnell to talk with them. He'd already given the media the bare facts he was allowed to disclose, but they knew Parnell would not publicize the name of the murder victim until the next of kin had been notified. A newspaper photographer took dozens of pictures of the rowboat, the ferry office and the patch of blood on the walkway.

After the coroner, the first person allowed to touch the body, handed over the contents of Todd's pockets to a detective, he pronounced the corpse ready to be transported to the morgue. The police photographer packed up his equipment and left. Only two officers, still holding back the press, and Parnell remained. At his side was Jim Salocco, owner of the ferry company.

"Detective, you don't need a warrant to go inside. I own this building, and you're welcome to inspect it."

"Thanks, Mr. Salocco, but I'd rather wait for an official warrant. We need to do this by the book. You might change your mind once we're in there and find something. That's happened to us before. Besides, as far as we know, there's never been a murder on Isabel Island, and we've already received a few angry phone calls from residents."

Salocco nodded his head. "Not surprising. The people who live right on the waterfront are wealthy. As you know, the prices of these houses start at five million. They won't like the thought of a murder on their doorstep."

Parnell sighed. "That's why we have to make sure we catch whoever struck the poor kid down as fast as possible. I hope it isn't an owner of one of the fancy yachts tied up here." The two men looked down the length of the island. The smallest berthed vessel was a thirty-five-foot sailboat.

He turned his attention to the rowboat, asking Salocco, "Do you know who it belongs to? And how about those other three pulled up on the sand?"

"No. I have no idea. Can't help you there. I guess they all belong to the homeowners. A few of them leave their small rowboats and dinghies on the sand all the time."

The detective thanked him and went to tell the two cops to start knocking on doors for possible witnesses and to ask about ownership of the rowboat. He knew it was doubtful anyone had heard or seen anything. According to the medical examiner the crime apparently occurred between midnight and three a.m., at which time the detective figured most of the residents would have been sleeping. The Harbor Patrol had been of no help. They reported they'd neither seen nor heard anything out of the ordinary during their routine nightly inspection of the bay.

"Anything more you can tell us, detective?" asked one of the reporters.

"Not yet. We'll know the cause of death soon, and you can stop by the station for our initial report. It won't tell you much, though. The crime occurred in the early hours of the morning, and right now we have no witnesses."

Finally the press left. The police packed up their gear, the yellow tape was taken down, and Parnell ordered his men back to the station. The helicopters had long since departed, and as the police got into their squad cars and drove away, the residents who remained went silently back to their homes.

The following day Detective Parnell sat opposite J.J. and Tosca at their dining table, finding a space for his notebook between a teapot and two cups and saucers. Nice cozy cottage, he thought, looking around. The daughter was obviously still a bit shook up, but her mother seemed to be handling the situation just fine.

He tugged at his tie. A clean-shaven man of forty-four with a receding hairline, he disliked having to wear a suit. Too bad the Newport Beach police chief believed his detectives should present a professional appearance to Isabel Island's next-door millionaires who were a dime a dozen, even in the failing economy.

"Thank you for coming to the station yesterday, Mrs. Trevant, and giving us your fingerprints and statement," said Parnell. "I need to clear up a few more details, if you don't mind. Tell me again how you came to be at the scene of the crime."

"That poor young man. It's such a tragedy. All right, all right, officer. Calm down. I'm getting to it. As I told you before I was taking my usual early morning walk around the entire perimeter of the island which, I'm told, is three miles if you also count the Little Island."

"Mother, the detective only needs the relevant facts."

"Distance is very relevant, especially in crime scenes." Tosca turned her attention back to Parnell. "Isn't that right, chief inspector?"

"It's detective, ma'am. Please continue."

"A young woman was jogging toward me," said Tosca. "Such long legs American girls have. Before she got close I saw her suddenly veer onto the beach toward a small boat that was pulled up there. The woman beckoned me over."

Tosca paused to drink her tea.

"Please go on, Mrs. Trevant," said Parnell.

"Well, when she called out to me, she was laughing. 'You have to see this,' she said when I approached. 'Someone went to bed drunk and forgot to tuck themselves completely in.' And with that she took off jogging again."

"Yes. Did you get her name?"

"No, she ran off. I told you that. Anyway, I went right up to the boat to see what she was talking about, because of course I didn't want to seem stand-offish, especially since she'd turned around to see if I'd gone to take a look."

"Not," interjected J.J., "that my mother needs any encouragement to be nosy. She's a gossip columnist, after all."

Parnell ignored the daughter. "Please go on, Mrs. Trevant. Tell me again what you saw."

"The boat had a canvas cover."

"Yes, yes, but I need you to elaborate. Go on!" said Parnell.

"Elaborate? You want details? Certainly. The boat cover on this rowboat was brown canvas with white stitching. Badly sewn, obviously a rush job. You'd never see that in England, you know."

Detective Parnell winced. The next time the Brits went to war they could darned well watch out for themselves. "Please continue," he said.

"I saw the lower part of a bare leg hanging over the side of the boat from under the boat cover. The leg obviously belonged to someone wearing boat shoes, and I would certainly hope he was wearing shorts. I supposed the jogger was correct. It was just some drunk college kid or perhaps a homeless person looking for a bed, poor thing."

Parnell saw Tosca look at J.J., who was scowling back at her mother. Was the woman hiding something? She sure looked guilty.

"Then what did you do?" asked Parnell.

"I closed my parasol and put it carefully down on the sand. It's from China. You know, I thought that the leg looked pale, even bluish. I've seen dead bodies before, and this looked like it could be one. I decided to pull the canvas cover back to take a look, but when I crouched down to do that the leg started swinging, and the person's foot came around, knocking my sunglasses off. Yes, I know it was early in the morning, but Brits are not used to such dazzling sunlight, you see."

The detective suppressed a smile. He'd have given a lot to have been there. "Please go on, ma'am."

"Anyway, after the shoe hit me it came off his foot and dropped onto the sand right in front of me. The shoe fell on its side, and a shiny silver coin rolled out."

Tosca went on to describe how she'd finally got the cover off the boat and seen the body, its head covered in blood.

"So I immediately got out my mobile, my iPhone, and called 911. But then the jogger came back, saw me still standing next to the boat and came over. As soon as she saw the blood, she took out her phone, too. I hope she wasn't calling the tabloids. Not that calling the press is a bad thing. I work for a tabloid myself, you know, but it's in England. Have you ever heard of 'Tiara Tittle-Tattle?'"

Parnell shook his head. He felt like laughing, but murder was a serious business, and according to the medical examiner's initial evaluation the kid had been hit with a metal bar or something similar. Judging by the amount of blood from the head wound on the boardwalk outside the door of the ferry office, that's where the killing had occurred.

However, the head injury wasn't responsible for his death. The coroner had already determined the cause to be strangulation. Bruises in the shape of fingers were evident on the victim's neck. Parnell knew that the thyroid gland in Todd's neck would have ruptured, collapsing the carotid artery. Meaning, he thought, that the killer has strong hands. He knew that if the artery is closed for between eight and fourteen seconds, unconsciousness and death occurs. Squeezing a healthy young man's neck for that period of time took strength and endurance, someone with a powerful grip. There were no scratches on the neck, indicating that the murderer's nails were probably clipped short.

Parnell looked again at the investigating team leader's report.

"Let's get back to the silver coin you found. Was it just one?" he said.

"Yes," said Tosca, her guilty expression returning. "A single coin. I gave it to the other detective. The lettering on it is Greek. I'm sure you know that. Obviously the dead person was hiding the coin in his shoe.

"Why didn't you leave it there?"

"Because, my man, it rolled out onto the sand as the shoe fell off the foot. Two seagulls were poking around nearby. One tried to grab the coin with his beak, but I beat him to it. American gulls are very aggressive, aren't they? But very clean. I thought the coin was a dime at first. I just love your money, it's so much lighter than ours."

Used to be worth a whole lot more than yours, too, thought Parnell sourly. "Are you aware you are not supposed to touch anything at a crime scene, or worse still, remove anything?"

"Officer, I expect to be promoted to crime reporter when I return to England, so of course I know the rules."

"Then why did you pick it up?"

If she gives me one more of those guileless gazes of hers I swear I'll take her in, Parnell decided. "Well, ma'am?"

"I thought the seagull was going to swallow it, poor thing. They'll eat anything, you know. "

Sure thinks quick on her feet, I'll give her that, he thought. But seagulls aren't stupid enough to eat metal.

"Was it checked for fingerprints?" said Tosca.

"Oh yes, we found fingerprints on the coin, as well as on the side of the boat and the shoe. Did you touch anything else, ma'am?"

"Of course not. So whose prints were they?"

"Yours, of course." He watched a slow blush cover Tosca's cheeks.

"No one else's?"

"No, ma'am, your prints pretty much obliterated our chances of finding any others."

FOURTEEN

Back at the police station Parnell opened one of the file cabinets in the Records Department and pulled out a thin folder under the name Gustave Vernays. The detective knew the Swiss coin dealer had a reputation for being on the fringe of the world's small group of superstar fences although, in spite of rumors to the contrary, he'd never been actually caught receiving or selling stolen goods.

Known to Interpol as a top numismatist and one they'd like to arrest for dealing in ancient coins stolen from museums and archeological sites, Vernays managed to slip through their fingers at every turn, as the agency acknowledged.

For his part Parnell knew that the Swiss man did not consider himself a common fence but more of a broker of high-end merchandise that had historic connections. Moreover, many of his transactions were legitimate, and occasionally he was consulted by law enforcement authorities to authenticate items they had collected as evidence in criminal cases they were pursuing. Fortunately for us, the detective mused, he's local, and we have him right here. He's sure to be able to identify this Greek thing. A visit was in order. After checking Vernays' address, he drove north to Anaheim Hills.

"Definitely Greek but maybe not an original," Gustave Vernays told Parnell, staring at the coin encased in a small see-through evidence bag. He delicately turned the bag over to study the other side as the detective watched the man's face for any hint that he recognized the coin that had fallen from the boy's shoe.

Parnell asked if they could sit at the small dining table, and the two sat down. The detective produced a notebook and pen.

"I need to clear up a couple of things, Mr. Vernays. The kid's parents are devastated, of course. They arrived from Minnesota today. We've talked to his friends and a few fellow students at Saddleback College, as well as his roommate and others. We thought he might be a coin collector, but that was not the case."

"If his parents want to meet me, I'm agreeable."

"No, no," Parnell said quickly. "I doubt that will be necessary. However, I need to get one or two specifics from you. For instance, do you know anyone local who might have owned this coin? How about giving me a list of your collectors who buy Greek coins?"

Vernays reacted as if hit. "Names? Detective, I cannot possibly provide that confidential information. I'm like a doctor, a lawyer. My clients would have my head if I revealed who they are. Public knowledge of their valuable collections would put them at risk. No, Detective Parnell, out of the question."

"You forget, sir, that this is a murder investigation. We can easily get a warrant."

"All right. I can ask my clients if they would agree to talk to you, but most of them live in other countries, and what could they know?"

The afternoon sun filtered through the ivory silk chiffon curtains, casting a soft light onto everything it touched. Sumptuous quarters, Parnell thought. Lucky guy to be able to work at home. Guess he keeps his merchandise in a safe, but there's no sign of one in this room—in fact, no sign that any business at all is conducted here. Pretty high-class décor. He looked around at the oil paintings and the small bronze sculptures sitting in lighted alcoves. The aura of wealth was palpable. Why, Parnell wondered, doesn't this guy move to exclusive Newport Coast or the quiet wealth of Dana Point? Anaheim Hills had its pricey enclaves, sure, but it wasn't his idea of splendor, way inland and hot as hell in the summer. If it were me, I'd be living right down at beachside next to the ocean.

"Where did you get it?" Vernay's words cut into Parnell's thoughts.

"Can't tell you that, sir, but it could be involved in the case." If this guy knows anything about the murder on Isabel Island and can tell me who the coin belonged to, he's hiding it well, thought the detective. The dealer's face was expressionless.

"Silver, of course," he said. "It's an aegina, one of the first European coins to be struck in the seventh century B.C. I can remove it from the bag, yes?"

"Yes, sir," said Parnell.

After Vernays took the coin out his fingertips gently caressed the slightly raised, worn-down design. "You can barely see it, but that's a turtle on this side, which was later replaced by a tortoise."

Parnell's gaze sharpened. Did the man know the history of this particular coin? Could he have been conducting a midnight sale at the beach and dropped it? Hardly likely, and he sure isn't a surfer, though he was lean enough.

"Really?" said the detective. "This is my first hands-on introduction to the world of precious coins, and you've captured my curiosity. Why a turtle first, then a tortoise?"

"One theory is that the turtle symbolized the Greek goddess of love, Aphrodite, so the coin design paid homage to her. Chinese scholars, however, claim the first minted coins copied the shells of turtles and tortoises and were used as currency in parts of China."

"Aphrodite? I thought Venus was the goddess of love," said Parnell.

"Venus is the Roman version of Aphrodite. In other parts of the world she was known as Ishtar and Astarte, not very beautiful names."

"So what else can you tell me about this coin? Who would have owned it? Is it worth big bucks? Was it stolen? Would someone kill to possess it?"

The detective could see that Vernays was in a quandary. Admit to its value and origin, such as a museum, and Interpol could become involved.

"I've no idea who may have owned it," Vernays told the detective. "A collector most likely, I suppose, but none of my acquaintance. But then, there are collectors who are very secretive. As to its value, that's hard to say. It looks ancient, yes, but it could be a copy, in which case no one would dream of killing for it. Leave it with me, detective, and I'll run some tests on it."

Parnell snatched up the coin. "No, thanks, sir, We can do our own tests. Appreciate your help. Let us know if anything occurs to you regarding a possible owner and provenance."

The detective returned the small coin to its evidence bag and said goodbye. Downstairs, he got back into his squad car and drove to Isabel Island. Much as he disliked the idea, he realized he needed another session with the woman who'd found the aegina, congratulating himself for remembering how to pronounce its name.

Parnell phoned Tosca from his squad car and said he'd like to stop by.

"What, again? Officer, sheriff, chief, detective, whichever you are, I really don't think there's anything more I can tell you," said Tosca. "We've talked twice already."

"Mrs. Trevant, you've probably forgotten a few details. That's understandable with anyone finding a dead body. It must have been pretty shocking for someone like you who has just arrived here, but the first twenty-four hours are crucial to our investigation. I won't keep you long." He quickly ended the call and within ten minutes was at her house.

The top half of the door was open, and he saw her on the sofa, working on a laptop and surrounded by piles of paper. At the sound of the chimes, she looked up, smiled, set aside the computer and came to the door, opening the lower half.

"Do come in."

Seated again with the detective facing her in an armchair, she inquired as to the progress of the investigation.

"The victim has been identified," said Parnell, "but we've hit a wall for a suspect or suspects. It could have been a robbery gone wrong. That's one possibility as the day's takings were found in a bank bag on the floor of the ferry office. Maybe the murderer was interrupted before he could grab the bag."

"If that were the case," said Tosca, "why take the time to hide the body in the boat? Why not just flee the scene?"

"We believe the killer came back later to do that."

"Yes," said Tosca, "pretty obvious. I noticed the trail of blood leading to the boat was fresher than the stain on the boardwalk, indicating that the body had lain where it had fallen before being moved. I assume he was a student?"

"He went to Saddleback College, working his way through school with a job on the ferry."

Tosca offered the detective a drink, and he opted for water. She poured herself a small glass of mead and sat back down. "All right. So what are the new questions you have for me?"

"You seem to be a pretty observant lady. Have you noticed anyone strange on Isabel Island?" Aside from yourself, he refrained from adding.

He could see she appeared to be considering the question carefully before answering.

"Frankly, detective, as you know, I am a newcomer here. There are cultural differences that strike me as odd, but to you they'd be quite normal, and I respect that. So, no, I can't say I've noticed anyone strange, certainly not anyone a Brit would consider eccentric. We've a ton of those back home. I think some of the neighbors find me a little unusual when they hear me swear in Cornish, but I use very mild swear words. My parasol, too, seems to evoke comment."

Parnell consulted his notebook. Maybe he should quit while he was ahead. Her formal manner of speaking was getting to him. Two more questions, and I'm out of here, he decided.

"Are you sure there was only one coin in the boy's shoe? I know you told us so, but please think back. It's a Greek coin, an aegina, by the way. "

"Really? Are you a numismatist?"

"Uh, I consulted a local coin collector, Gustave Vernays. Are you sure, Mrs. Trevant, there weren't more coins?"

"Just the one, detective. I'm positive. Did you examine the other shoe and the toe part of both?"

"Yes. Nothing."

"Did you find fingerprints in the ferry office?"

"No. Everything was wiped clean."

"Who does that coin belong to?"

"Still working on it." Parnell found himself answering the questions she threw at him before realizing he shouldn't have. He flipped his notebook closed and stood up to leave.

"Detective, I would really like to look at your report," said Tosca. "I can come along to the police station right now."

"Sorry, ma'am. The file is confidential. Thanks for your help."

He ran down the outside steps as fast as he could, got into his car and headed for the police station, breathing a sigh of relief.

After Detective Parnell left, Tosca returned to her laptop. She'd already worked on the scene of the ferry boat crime for the article she intended to send to her editor. Perhaps Stuart will take me more seriously now, she thought. He'll surely promote me to crime reporter right here in America, but first I have to solve the puzzle of the finger bones. Shouldn't be that difficult. All I have to do is what I've done for years, snoop around and figure it out. Stuart will appreciate the fact that Newport Beach and Isabel Island, with their reputation as playgrounds for millionaires, are the perfect setting for a nasty murder.

The seafront homes, the expensive yachts, the chic boutiques, exclusive tennis, golf, and sailing clubs, and the ritzy restaurants will all intrigue him as the backdrop for a killing. When she'd traveled to the private West Indies island of Mustique for the first time to cover Princess Margaret's vacation there and later Prince William's visit, her editor had impressed upon her the need to describe Mustique's exotic, tropical beauty for her readers,.

But she'd also written about its seamier side and discovered she was fascinated with the criminal element. Now, on a platter, she had just been handed the golden opportunity to further her ambition by reporting on not one but possibly two crimes. But although the ferry boat fare-taker was a definite murder, and the skeleton fingers in Professor Whittaker's garden needed to be sorted out, she was still worried about the royal lawsuit.

Her editor's earlier email had been unnerving. "We have our solicitors talking to the palace again this week. Is there anything else you've neglected to tell me about what was going on in that room on the fourth floor? Are you positive about whom you saw? What a bloody mess."

"Stuart," Tosca wrote back, "of course I am positive. Don't be ridiculous. I've seen the royals often enough to know who's who. It's not my fault I opened the wrong door. The footman pointed one out and then scuttled off like a scared mouse. Now look, I am involved in figuring out not one but two murders here. You'll have a story soon. Toodle-oo, love."

She continued to tinker with her description of Isabel Island, adding a few historical details about the decades-old ferry and its daily trips across the sheltered bay. She wrote a paragraph on the stately palm trees shipped in from Fiji, thought by tourists to be home grown, and she composed a few sentences praising the nearby mountains and canyons while noting that the lack of rain kept them more golden than green.

Tosca described the students who took summer jobs as surf instructors, busboys and lifeguards, how the ferry boat murder was the first to be committed on the enchanting island, and the luxury lifestyle of Newport Beach. Her words painted a stark contrast between the beauty of the bay and the horror of the crime, but Tosca knew she couldn't write more until she found out what the police had discovered.

She decided to send the half-finished draft to Stuart right away and get his comments. He answered almost immediately.

"Why would our newspaper be interested in murders in America?" he wrote. "They have dozens every day, I understand, especially in Los Angeles."

"Not with England's top gossip columnist hot on the trail, " Tosca wrote back. "I am personally involved in the case."

"All right, all right. Don't get your dander up. Let me know when you've brought the murderer to heel.

Shouldn't take you more than a day or two, the way you jump to conclusions."

After reading her editor's sarcastic words, Tosca closed the email connection and went back to ponder a dilemma. She needed to visit the police station and take a look at the police file. Maybe she should take some mead with her, debating whether they'd consider it a bribe. It might be a waste of her good wine. Even if it were appreciated, they'd probably never heard of mead. She hadn't seen any mention of mead on a restaurant's wine menu or at a bar.

Looks like I'll have to make a new batch, she decided, a different recipe this time. Closer to twelve percent alcohol rather than the usual fourteen percent.

FIFTEEN

Whittaker finally received the phone call he was anxiously awaiting from coin broker Gustave Vernays.

"You're in luck, Professor. Two collectors, one in Spain and another in Dubai, are interested, but the bids are much lower than I expected."

"I want top dollar. What are you trying to do, give it away for nothing? You told me it would take a long time, and here you have a couple of offers already. Keep trying. Keep trying." Whittaker crashed the phone's handset back into its cradle.

Damn, my blood pressure's going through the roof again, he fumed as he waddled into the garage and grabbed a rake, a shovel and a bucket. As he made his way to the front yard he was reminded of the summer he was eight years old.

"What are you doing with that dead rabbit?" his cousin Betty, two years younger, had asked the first time they spent their summer school vacation together at her parents' ranch in Arizona. "Don't touch it. It could be full of germs. I'm going to tell on you."

Without answering, Haiden had carried the creature into the barn and, for no reason he could explain, suddenly chopped off its paws with what he assumed was a tomahawk but was actually a hatchet hanging on the wall. Betty screamed and ran off, calling her mother. Fortunately, dear sweet Aunt Lillian hadn't been able to believe such a horror, Whittaker remembered. He'd used a shovel to bury the rabbit under some hay before his aunt came into the barn. The tiny paws were in his pocket, dripping a small amount of blood.

That night he washed the pocket linings of his shorts and hung the clothing on the windowsill to dry. Before he went to bed he'd taken his Play-Doh from its plastic bag and encased the animal's paws in the soft clay, rolling them into tennis-sized balls. Since then he'd acquired other dead animals' paws with which to fashion sculptures and ornaments. He knew he wasn't the first to indulge in such macabre behavior; and in any case, he reminded himself, Stone Age hunters made weapons, tools, trinkets and vessels from skeletal remains. In 2007 a gravedigger in Fitchburg, Massachusetts, stole human bones to fashion into ashtrays. What did the man call it, recycling? The professor chuckled quietly. Who could argue with that? And what does my own little quirk make me?

His victims had all been animals, of course. It had never occurred to him to kill a person until he was talking to Dr. Joel Bernstein a few months before Monica died.

"Look at this, Haiden," Bernstein had remarked a couple of months earlier, holding up a tiny glass vial.

They were in the pharmacology lab at the University of California, Irvine. Bernstein's daughter, a promising cellist, played in the school orchestra and had taken private lessons from the professor. Once or twice, like today, Whittaker had felt free to ask Bernstein, a chemist, for his opinion about certain acids for cleaning the coins in his collection.

He peered at the glass vial the doctor was unwrapping from a large box on the counter.

"What is it?" he asked.

"Death." Bernstein shook the small container filled with a translucent bluish liquid before repacking it in its plastic cover and replacing it carefully into the box with dozens of similar vials. "It just arrived. Liquid morphine, derived from opium. Mix several drops with some strong booze, and poof, you're at heaven's gate."

"Is that what those thirty-nine suicides swallowed?" Whittaker asked, referring to a group of cult members who had killed themselves in San Diego because they were convinced a spaceship awaited them.

"No. They took phenobarbital capsules along with liquor. That's what did the trick. Mix this pretty juice with booze, too, and you'll get the same result, and it would be invisible if you used it in, say, a blue or green liqueur. Now what was your question?"

"Ammonia. If I use it to remove the oxide from this coin, will it damage the surface?" Whittaker passed a Turban Head one-cent piece enclosed in a small plastic bag to Bernstein, who took it and turned it from side to side.

"Actually, Haiden, you're talking about a hydroxide solution, the same thing dry cleaners use, so it shouldn't do any harm unless someone ingests it. Let me look it up to be sure. I'll be right back," he said, returning the coin envelope to Whittaker.

As soon as Dr. Bernstein went into his office next door, the professor peered into the packing case that contained the vials of morphine. He took a vial from the box, removed it from its plastic wrap and slipped it into his trouser pocket. Haiden stuffed the empty slot in the box with the packing material. Impulse again, he supposed, but the doctor's words had given him the germ of an idea, and as long as the vial was not missed he'd be home free.

The doctor came back into the room smiling. "You're safe. Go ahead and use the hydroxide. It should give that coin a nice clean surface." He turned to the box of morphine and closed its lid. "Better get these locked up. Students nick all kinds of stuff around here, looking for a cheap thrill."

SIXTEEN

Tosca was surprised to receive a phone call from Thatch almost as soon as he'd left her house. He'd decided, he said, that he'd like to take a look himself at Haiden Whittaker's yard. From the sidewalk, of course. Was it convenient to return?

Guess he thinks there's something dodgy going on after all, Tosca mused. Or, being retired from the U.S. Secret Service, maybe he's planning to set up his own private detective agency. Well, I'll see about that. This is my criminal case, and I'm not about to share it with anyone.

She quickly changed into a pink and lavender cotton sundress. Not too dressy but feminine, she decided. She added purple amethyst and silver clip-on earrings and pale gray high-heeled shoes.

When Thatch arrived she again poured two glasses of mead. He was obviously anxious to get down to business, as she noticed he ignored the drink. Placing his Stetson upside down on the coffee table, as before, and sitting on the sofa, he said, "I have to persuade my FBI friend that the rock you gave me is something special. So I need to see its exact location. I have a pretty good idea what it is, but I'm not going to say right now."

"Why not?" said Tosca. "It's fingertips, isn't it?"

He grinned at her. "Be patient."

"All right, you win. You can drink the mead later." Tosca nodded at his untouched glass. "Come with me." Unabashedly she took his hand and gave a little tug to pull him off the sofa. He picked up his hat.

"Oh, I knew I wanted to ask you something. Why do you place your cowboy hat upside down when you take it off?"

"Gravity. Keeps the brim curved up."

Well, he certainly doesn't waste words, she thought. His explanation made sense, though she'd never seen a cowboy do that in a Western movie.

"Are you a native Californian?" she asked.

"No, ma'am. I'm from Wyoming and a Cornhusker."

Tosca stood still for a moment, frowned, then said, "Sorry. What's does that mean, that you eat mainly corn?"

Thatch let out a booming laugh. "Means I went to the University of Nebraska-Lincoln and played on the football team. I was a linebacker, and sure, I do eat plenty of corn. I'm a vegetarian. Now how about we get along to this professor's house?"

They walked toward Whittaker's garden.

"There's a second rock exactly like the one I gave you," said Tosca, "but it's smooth and unbroken." As they slowed their steps a few yards from the professor's gate she whispered, "It's on top of the little shrine he has at the rear, against the wall in what he calls a rock garden. The plants around it are high, but you might be able to see it."

As they approached the fence, she drew in a breath."Oh, no! He's weeded," she said in disgust, "and dismantled the rock garden."

"'And sune thou shalt be thrown aside, like any common weed and vile,'" Thatch quoted as the two stood outside Whittaker's gate for a few seconds.

Tosca grinned. "So you know your Rabbie Burns," she said. "Not my favorite poet, but I'd never say that in Scotland. Well, we might as well go home. We could finish the mead."

Thatch's cell rang. He listened, then said, "Sorry, have to make tracks. I'll call you soon."

"And to think," said Tosca back in J.J.'s kitchen, slicing tomatoes, "he quoted that old drunkard Burns to me. Besides which I found out Thatch is a vegetarian. A strapping big chap like that! He said he's from Wyoming. Isn't that full of cattle ranches? Must be steaks galore there."

"He quoted Burns? Well, well, so he has a soft side." J.J. gave her mother a wide smile. "When am I going to meet this man that has attracted your attention so much?"

"I wouldn't have minded if he'd chosen one of the more obscure poets like Artur Dall MacGurcaigh," said Tosca, "or even a modern one like Aonghas MacNeacail. Why are you laughing?" She turned toward J.J. who was convulsed in giggles.

"Those names are hysterical. Did you make them up?"

"Of course not, but they're Scottish Gaelic, not Cornish Gaelic, so what do you expect? Let's have dinner. The salad's ready."

SEVENTEEN

As Thatch drove away from the Trevant apartment he felt like kicking himself for quoting Robert Burns. He usually kept his love of poetry under wraps in public. Only his immediate family knew he had an entire bookcase devoted to his passion for the Romantic period. He treasured his volumes of Keats, Shelley, Byron and other eighteenth century poets. Thatch had to agree with Tosca, though. Burns wasn't even close to being among his favorites. Still, the line fit perfectly, and he hadn't been able to resist, considering her constant use of Cornish.

I bet my Great-granddad Murchadh would have understood her language, he thought. The old man had spoken fluent Gaelic, and Thatch remembered Grandpa Niall, too, speaking it as head of the MacAulay clan in the Scottish Highlands. Niall had sent Andrew, his eldest son, to America. Andrew landed in New York, hated its crowded, dirty streets and immediately set off for points west, where the mountain ranges and wide open prairies were more to his liking, reminding him of home.

Almost starving to death after a stint as a gold miner for the Carissa Mine, which soon went bust, Andrew MacAulay settled in northwest Wyoming as a homesteader. There was no fortune to be made from the hardscrabble land, but he survived, raised a family and died at the age of one hundred two.

The American MacAulays eventually lost touch with their Scottish ancestors, but Thatch enjoyed the romantic notion that he himself was probably a laird. It had been a family joke when the kids were growing up. "Maybe we'll take a trip to Scotland one day and claim our heritage," he'd tell them. They would always laugh and say, "When, when?"

Of course, they'd never made the journey. Life had intervened. Now, as Thatch let himself into his rambling ranch-style house on a small lot halfway up a bluff overlooking Newport Beach's Back Bay, his curiosity about his roots returned. Yes, definitely a trip to Scotland or maybe Cornwall with a visit to a couple of those meaderies Tosca talked about, he thought, walking out to his favorite spot, the flagstone patio.

He'd bought the house seven years ago when his wife Barbara came home from the hospital, the cancer diagnosed as terminal. She'd refused to spend her final few weeks in the sterile environment of a hospice, wanting to say goodbye to her husband, son and daughter on her own terms. Thatch signed on with a twenty-four-hour nursing agency to care for her. His boss at the Secret Service Agency had been understanding, telling him to take as much time as he needed. As it turned out, Barbara succumbed only a month later. After settling his wife's estate he'd offered the house to his children, but they had preferred to make their own living arrangements. Thatch rented it out until taking his retirement and moving back in.

At first he'd thought its memories would be too painful, the rooms empty and echoing; but the children persuaded him to stay there, and now he was glad he had. The patio overlooked the waters of the bay where over the centuries the Santa Ana River had cut a wide swath, carving out towering white cliffs. Designated an ecological and wildlife preserve, the bay was in constant motion, with habitats hosting red-tailed hawks and other birds cruising the thermals; sandpipers, egrets and black rails. In the salt marsh were jackknife clams, and in the freshwater ponds, crayfish.

Thatch took a beer from the refrigerator, settled himself into a well-worn rattan rocker, took a pull on the beer can and closed his eyes. Listening to the calls of the birds, he had come to identify most of them, but the harsh cawing of the crows and the screeching of the seagulls never failed to perturb him. They always seemed agitated and restless, and he tried to ignore them.

His cell phone rang. "Thatch, Dan. Just confirming tomorrow. Looking forward to it."

"Me too, See you there."

Thatch arrived early at Shaunessey's pub for his lunch appointment with FBI Special Agent Dan Delano. He ordered two Stiegl beers at the bar and carried them to a table in a small alcove toward the rear of the restaurant. He put his satchel on the floor, sat down and set one of the beers opposite him. Across the room he recognized a couple of agents from the local FBI field office, where Delano was Assistant Director in Charge.

The FBI's Los Angeles headquarters enjoyed crime jurisdiction over a population of eighteen million people and had field offices in seven counties in Southern California. Federal, state and city law enforcement agency personnel were a relatively small group, and many knew each other from various cases on which they'd collaborated.

Thatch nodded almost imperceptibly at the agents when their eyes met. He knew they knew he was ex-Secret Service, recently retired.

Taking his first sip of beer, he didn't notice Delano arrive but acknowledged his presence after being slapped hard on the shoulder. A portly man in his mid-forties, reaching close to six feet, Delano was known for the wide grin that split his homely face almost in two. Who wouldn't like a guy who smiles with such genuine warmth? Thatch recalled his wife saying.

"Hey, you remembered my favorite brew," said Delano, sitting down opposite Thatch, setting a backpack on the floor, and nodding at the glass of beer on his side of the table. "Ready?"

Both men raised their glasses, chanting in unison, *"Es muss ein Stiegl sein!"*

After they drank deeply of the Austrian beer, Thatch grinned and said, "So old age hasn't caught up with you yet. You still remember the beer slogan we learned in Salzburg. But I can't believe you've held on to that ratty old backpack you bought in Morocco."

Delano smiled, took a quick look around the pub, nodded at the agents he recognized, then turned his attention back to his friend. "Been a while, Thatch, since we talked. How are you enjoying retirement?"

"Busier than I thought it'd be, to tell you the truth. I figured on having to buy a recliner and a plasma TV. But as you know, I'm an outdoors guy, and this geology hobby has blossomed into kind of a full-time occupation."

"You don't miss the Service?" said Delano. "Although I have to say I never envied you being at the sharp end of the spear, as you guys call it, and being on call twenty-four/seven. We're used to surveillance, but I doubt I could keep such constant vigilance on a President of the United States without going nuts. So as I said, do you miss all that good stuff?"

"At first I did, sure, the daily briefings, the threat assessments, the highs of protecting the President, even the stress of the assignments, but that's history now. Even the shoe-throwing incident in Iraq with President Bush." He stopped to nod at Delano's downturned mouth. "Yeah, I know. We were slow off the mark there. Didn't react till the second shoe came flying through the air. Great aim, that journalist had. I guess shoe throwing is an art form in the Middle East. You hold it by the toe. The guy hurled both shoes with perfect accuracy." He paused to grimace at the memory. "But that's old news. One thing I did enjoy at retirement was donating the formal dark suits, the boring ties and those Hollywood-style dark sunglasses to charity. As you can see, I now live in jeans."

"Well, it's great to see you again. I've been meaning to get in touch, but you know how it is," said Delano as a waitress came over to take their order. "You still a vegetarian, Thatch?"

"Absolutely, though I haven't progressed to being a strict vegan, and I doubt I ever will." Turning to the waitress, he said, "I'll take the cheese lasagna."

After Delano ordered beef stroganoff, and the waitress left, he said, "Fill me in on your life: Not remarried, are you?"

Thatch regarded his friend for a moment before replying. "Dan, this isn't exactly a social lunch, though I'm glad to see you. You must have wondered why I asked you to bring your briefcase. I'm kind of working on something." At Delano's surprised expression he added quickly, "Strictly unofficially. I'm just doing a favor for a friend. It's an oddball thing, possibly a crime."

Reaching into the satchel he'd put under the table, Thatch brought out the rock and set it on the table between them. He turned it so that the broken-off side faced Delano, who said, "One of your geology finds?"

Thatch ignored the question. "Dan, see these little things sticking out? I'd like an analysis of exactly what they are."

"Fossils?"

"Yeah. Maybe. Some kind. This so-called stone isn't an actual stone, but that's all I want to say right now. I know exactly what the composition is, but I'd like an official report, if you can swing it for me. Andy's already opened a file jacket at the Newport Police Department, so we're official, sort of."

"You want a lab test?"

"Sure do. Your Bureau's forensic services are much more extensive than ours. The Secret Service focuses more on counterfeit and financial matters, questionable documents, fingerprint and voice identification, and polygraphs."

"True," said Delano. "Your polygraph programs are phenomenal, and I know your ink library is unsurpassed. I was impressed with your old outfit when it started to provide forensic and technical help for missing and exploited children."

"I'm not asking for special treatment from you, but I sure as hell am curious, which makes me impatient."

"Jeez, Thatch, after all those years of learning to curb such emotions?"

"I know, I know. In a way it's a relief to be able to admit to them. So what do you say, can you handle it?"

"I'll find a way. I'm not an ADC for nothing. I think I have some pull at Quantico. Probably get it on a plane tonight. Hey, here's our lunch. Another round?"

EIGHTEEN

J.J. returned early from San Diego. After she and her mother had eaten a light supper, Tosca headed for the front door.

"Going for your evening walk?" J.J. got up from the dining table. "Maybe I'll come with you, or how about another driving lesson? We haven't taken the Healey out at night yet. I bet you've forgotten that the first gear is blocked off and has an overdrive, while the reverse gear is opposite to the usual configuration."

"No, thank you, dear. I have enough difficulty in broad daylight trying to find that silly little lump of wood that pretends it's a stick shift. Then there's the choke and the start button, to say nothing of driving down the wrong side of the road along these unlit streets."

"Mother, I've told you, it's easy, especially as the car has a left-hand drive, which is perfect for driving here in the States.

I must admit that unusual back-to-front gear pattern does take a bit of learning, though."

"Thanks, but again, no. I'm off to see the professor. I gave him a CD this afternoon. I want to see if he liked it."

J.J. shook her head. "You know, I think we should move to Iceland. Soon, like tonight."

Tosca laughed at her daughter's comment, picked up one of her jugs of mead, put it into her tote bag and left for Whittaker's house. Twilight was rapidly turning to night, the last faint rays of an orange sunset fading to gray. Boats sat silently at their moorings while one lone straggler, a small skiff, glided to a nearby dock. No breeze disturbed the sailboats this evening, free from the Santa

Ana winds that blew in from the desert and set halyards snapping loudly against their masts. Tonight all was quiet.

Before ringing Whittaker's bell Tosca paused to glance through his front window. Two brass standing lamps illuminated the room. Amazing, she thought, how no one on Isabel Island ever closed the drapes at night. During her evening walks she enjoyed staring through the windows at the lighted living rooms and making summary judgments on the owners' taste in furniture and art works. One would never see such a disregard for privacy in England, of course, Tosca sniffed.

Haiden was seated at the piano. She could faintly hear him playing Debussy's "Reverie." Overwhelmed by the sensitivity he brought to the fragile piece, Tosca stood listening on the doorstep for several moments, enthralled. In spite of his cold, strange behavior, this man couldn't possibly be a murderer, not with the tenderness his fingers on the keys revealed, she reflected. "These clumsy shells that house our souls may be cumbersome, but when we cast them off in death, they fall away to reveal the magnificence of our true glory," she quoted to herself, although she had long forgotten its source. How fitting the observation seemed to her now with regard to the professor.

Was she mistaken about him? Did he appear evil to her simply because of his "clumsy shell," his evasiveness, his dour manner? Surely these were not the qualities that determined a criminal mind. Quite the opposite, perhaps. After all, he'd just lost a wife. Maybe his soul was indeed pure, and Tosca was totally wrong and might be asked to leave America. She could just imagine how upset J.J. would be if that happened.

Yet, what about that round rock and the finger bones inside it? That was as damning as it could get, she thought. There is absolutely and positively a murder to be solved— two, in fact. What a story I'll have for my editor. She visualized huge apologies, demands that she return to the U.K., followed swiftly by an offer to take over the newspaper's top crime reporting spot. As for the royal lawsuit hanging over the *London Daily Post,* well, that would sort itself out eventually.

When the professor's playing stopped, and the final note died completely away, she was unwilling to shatter his mood with the strident ringing of the doorbell. Tosca decided to knock instead. The door swung back slowly, and the man's great bulk blocked the opening. Tosca noted his wary expression.

"Good evening, Haiden. Am I disturbing you? I was so moved by your playing. It brought tears to my eyes. Your delicate touch is perfection, bringing out the full pathos of the piece. I've never heard it played with such emotion."

Whittaker raised his eyebrows. "Well, well. Come in, come in, Tosca. I'm pleased you liked my playing." The professor continued talking as she entered the house. "Have you a favorite composition I can play for you? It would be my pleasure."

He led the way into the living room, where the stub of a blue candle smoldered in the bowl on the piano. Smiling, he stood seemingly transformed before her, his suspicion apparently giving way to surprise and joviality at her compliment.

"I was wondering," said Tosca as she settled herself into a corner of the sofa, "if you enjoyed the CD I brought you earlier, or haven't you had a chance to listen to it?"

"Not yet. Can I get you a cup of coffee?"

"Oh, no, thank you. I've brought you some of my Cornish mead." She took the small, corked jug from her purse.

"The glasses are in the kitchen." He picked up the jug and left the room.

Tosca looked around, again admiring the red brick fireplace and wondering if it was ever lit. Hanging above the mantel was a blue and red Tibetan thangka wall tapestry. This was a new addition since she was here last. Maybe now that Monica was gone, he felt free to indulge his own tastes.

As she turned to the opposite wall, her eyes stopped moving. She stood and walked quickly to the small antique picture frame hanging there, another new addition she hadn't seen before. Within its center, covered by glass, was a torn half-sheet of paper, part of a music score. On it were written two bars of music. As she studied its melody, Tosca recognized the unusual dissonant structure. Reading the musical arrangement carefully, she hummed it to herself. Beneath each note was a number, but she didn't understand how the numbers correlated to the musical notes.

"Ah!" said Whittaker, behind her. "I see you're interested in my twelve-tone row."

"Yes. Arnold Schoenberg, if I'm not mistaken."

Tosca noted his surprise.

"You are very perceptive," he said, "especially since the score is not signed. You know your music."

He set the half-filled wine glasses on the coffee table.

"Schoenberg was certainly a fiery, passionate composer," said Tosca. "I admire him greatly. To my mind, his "Verklärte Nacht" is the most haunting piece he ever wrote, yet it has been described as box office poison."

Whittaker took her arm. "Come and sit down, and we'll enjoy your mead."

Tosca resisted, continuing to study the piece. "What is the significance of those numbers?"

"Purely mathematical, dear lady, purely mathematical." He fluttered a dismissive hand. "Schoenberg is one of my idols, my favorite composer.

He once said the wonderful thing about music is that one can say everything in it, so that he who knows, understands everything,"

"Goodness, that's a cryptic comment if ever I heard one."

"He was a ritualistic man, a numerologist, as I am myself. Schoenberg attached numbers to letters of the alphabet to give them meaning. Those numbers, for instance," Whittaker pointed to the music score. "He might have used them for his students. He taught in Los Angeles. Piano teachers mark measures with numbers when they teach."

"Surely not the way these numbers are marked, professor?"

Whittaker shrugged. "As I said, the man loved numbers. It's common knowledge that when Schoenberg discovered his son's name, Roland, had adverse numerological implications, he changed the boy's name to Lawrence Adam. Did you know that the writing of music developed as artificial numbers in the late fifteenth century?"

"No," said Tosca. "My scholarship is far less broad than yours." At the professor's condescending smile, Tosca knew he was vain, too.

"Please, sit down." He took hold of Tosca's elbow again and led her back to the sofa. "I've never tasted mead."

"You're in for a treat," promised Tosca.

"It's certainly a strange color, Tosca, quite opaque."

"Yes, because of the honey and plants I use. It may look somewhat unappetizing, I'm afraid. In fact, J.J. won't get anywhere near it, but I think you'll find its robust flavor is most appealing to the palate."

The professor took a tentative sip. "You mentioned honey, but I didn't expect it to be this sweet. I like it. Thank you."

As they discussed Schoenberg, other composers and favorite pieces, she found herself appreciating Whittaker's vast musical knowledge until she heard his grandfather clock strike ten.

"It's late. I must go."

She thanked the professor for an enjoyable musical evening, told him to enjoy the rest of the mead she was leaving with him, bade him goodbye and left. As she passed the front of the house she was unable to resist her habit of peeking through undraped, lighted windows. She stopped abruptly when she saw him take the framed fragment of music off the wall, clutch it to his chest and hurry out of the room.

J.J., watching television in her favorite NASCAR T-shirt, was startled as her mother burst through the front door and planted herself dead center of the room, lips wide open in a triumphant smile.

"Looks like you had a successful visit," said J.J. "Well, don't just stand there grinning like the Cheshire Cat. Tell me what the professor said."

"There's absolutely something fishy going on. Oh, he was pleasant as could be, and we talked about music for ages, but then I asked him about a piece of sheet music he'd framed. It was hanging on the wall. He completely dismissed my question, but after I left I looked back through the window. You know how no one pulls their drapes around here. Well, I saw him take the frame off the wall. Can you imagine? I'd like to know why."

"What kind of music?" asked J.J.. "I listen to lots of different music and dance to it. So what's the big deal?"

"I doubt you'd be dancing to this, because no one can dance to twelve-tone compositions. Machines or robots, maybe. And you can't just listen to it. You have to figure it out while it's playing."

"Twelve-tone? Mother, you know I don't play the piano. That's complete gobbledygook to me. Keep it simple."

"All right. Arnold Schoenberg, an Austrian composer, decided that simply creating themes and developing them was too limiting. So instead, he decided that every single note of the twelve notes should have equal value. The only way he could do that was by not replaying a single note until every one of the twelve notes had been played and finished."

"Okay, I've got that. Is there more?"

"You'll like this bit. You can play the tone row backward, upside down, and even upside down and backward simultaneously."

"I may need a shot of whiskey to understand that."

"People usually do on first hearing it, but two rock musicians, Frank Zappa and Sid Vicious, both said they had been influenced by Schoenberg's atonal music."

"They're both dead," said J.J. "Maybe the challenge killed 'em off."

"Yes, well, so is Schoenberg's theory, basically. Anyway, to finish up, some of his compositions are considered too mathematical and even emotionless, but that's where Professor Whittaker's interest is, I believe, in the mathematical side of Schoenberg. Seems so to me, at any rate, considering those intriguing numbers added to the music he framed."

"Sorry I can't help you there, Mother. It's way over my head, and it's way past my bedtime. See you in the morning."

"Kosk yn da," said Tosca absentmindedly.

"Thanks. Sleep well yourself," replied J.J. She blew a kiss in her mother's direction and climbed the spiral staircase to bed.

Tosca, still puzzled by the professor's action, made herself another cup of tea, humming the notes she'd memorized from the framed page. Schoenberg's compositions were like abstract paintings, she'd read, and had turned the music world on its head when he'd first introduced it in his native Austria. Poorly received, Schoenberg's chamber symphonies and orchestral pieces were greeted by hisses and boos, but by the 1930s he was hailed as a genius. He immigrated to the United States and taught at the University of California, Los Angeles.

Tosca remembered from their conversation earlier in the evening that Haiden said there was a mathematical reason why he himself paid homage to Schoenberg. What could that be, and why did he now appear to be hiding the framed notes? Tosca found a notepad and pen in J.J.'s roll top desk and sat down to recreate the bars of music and numbers she'd seen.

She drew five horizontal lines to resemble a musical score sheet. Because of her photographic memory, which stood her in good stead as a reporter, she was able to visualize the notes and numbers, and copied them down. She was certain she recalled them correctly.

Opening up her laptop, she clicked on the Whittaker file and added the information to the notes for her article, unsure if the incident was of interest but encouraged to believe so because of Whittaker's actions. Why take the frame off the wall, and why only after Tosca commented on it? She needed to delve more deeply into Schoenberg's compositions.

NINETEEN

At breakfast the next morning J.J. proposed an hour's driving lesson. "You really must get the hang of it, Mother. That rental car is costing a fortune. A manual transmission is not that difficult to master. Once you learn to drive the Healey you can have it all to yourself when I'm away at the races."

"No time right now, love. I am off to the local library. I want to find a biography of Schoenberg. I need to know the significance of those numbers. Could they be the reason for the professor taking the music off the wall?"

J.J. shook her head. "Who knows? Now look, Mother, don't change the subject. You've been here almost three weeks already. When do you plan to get started learning how to drive my car?"

"*Ghas dha son.* Don't bully, dear, I've told you before, it's very unfeminine. Tell you what, why don't you drive me to the library, and I'll watch you shift gears on the way. I'll talk into my tape recorder and listen to the instructions later."

"All right, but I'm surprised you're still carrying around that recorder in your purse."

"Habit, I suppose. Besides, don't forget I'm writing a new column."

"Nothing from around here, I hope."

"Hardly, unless there's a princess or two hiding out down the street. Let's not worry about it. Come on, let's go."

Dressed in casual clothes, they set out. J.J. was in jeans, and Tosca reveled in wearing a cotton dress in the middle of February, a cold month back home in London.

At nine-thirty in the morning traffic off the island was light, most of its working inhabitants having left at least an hour earlier. Within minutes they were at the Newport Beach Public Library, an imposing building that had cost seventy-one million dollars, contributed largely by private donors. It was one of the larger libraries in Orange County and housed an exceptionally up-to-date and comprehensive reference section.

One of Tosca's first priorities after arriving in the United States had been to register for a library card. She became a frequent visitor to the newspaper racks, where she perused newspapers from around the world.

"Why bother?" said J.J. "It's all on the Internet."

"I like holding a real newspaper in my hands and turning the pages, flipping back if I need to and skipping sections instead of having to scroll down. It's still one of my great pleasures."

At the library Tosca swept past the newspaper racks this time and headed for the nonfiction book stacks while J.J. found an unoccupied computer and amused herself by searching for the latest online auto racing news. At the end of half an hour Tosca found what she needed among the biographies, selecting two on Schoenberg and three on other composers. She tapped J.J. on the shoulder to indicate they could leave and checked out the books she'd selected. They drove back to the island.

Tosca made tea for them both and delved into J. Peyser's *The New Music*. It confirmed that Schoenberg had indeed been a systematic person, a numerologist, basing many decisions in his life on the belief that numbers held specific implications, just as Professor Whittaker had told her. Schoenberg believed that the number thirteen stood for death. Rather than use it, he numbered his music measures 12 and 12A. He was convinced that he would die during a year that was a multiple of 13, but as it turned out, he was one year off.

Nevertheless, his death occurred on a fateful date: Friday, July 13, 1951.

After making some notes Tosca called the Newport Library information desk.

"I should have asked this while I was there earlier this morning. May I inquire as to where I would find original sheet music?"

"Modern or out of print?"

"Oh, definitely not modern. Classical pieces from the early nineteenth century."

"You could try the music department at the University of California, Irvine. They have archives and can probably help you out or give you some leads."

"Thank you so very much." Tosca closed her phone and called out to her daughter, who was sunbathing on the roof. "J.J., I'm going out. I'll drive my rental car."

Taking great care to keep the traffic dividing line on her left, all the while grumbling about uncivilized heathens who drove on the wrong side of the road, Tosca found her way to the library complex at the University of California, Irvine. Spread across fifteen hundred acres at the northern edge of Newport Beach, UCI was a major West Coast medical research university. It also boasted a thriving arts program; its symphony concerts and classic and modern plays were well attended. Professor Whittaker had obviously found a home.

The reference collection Tosca needed was in the Jack Langson Library, she was told, where the arts, humanities and other disciplines were housed. Given directions, Tosca approached the information desk and produced her copy of Professor Whittaker's Schoenberg music.

"May I speak to someone familiar with the music of Arnold Schoenberg, please?"

The young, blond librarian asked her to wait a moment. He went into the back office and returned with a woman who said she hoped she could help.

"Can you tell me which composition of Schoenberg's this is?" said Tosca.

The woman studied the sheet of paper for several moments. "I don't know all his orchestral scores. What are these numbers underneath the notes?"

"I was hoping you could tell me. Have you seen any of his original manuscripts like this? Did he ever write numbers on his pages? He was a numerologist, but I don't know if he simply doodled numbers on his scores or they really meant something." She asked if she could look at any Schoenberg archives that were available.

"We do have some," said the woman, "on the top floor. You'll need to show identification and a pass. Just a moment, please." She returned with a small cardboard ticket, told Tosca where the elevator was and instructed her to get out on the fourth floor.

Here the atmosphere was hushed. Showing her pass at yet another information desk, Tosca repeated her quest. She was shown to a small table and chair. A young man brought several large sheets of music and laid them before her. After he left she looked through them carefully. No numbers. She went back to the young man.

"Are there more archives?"

"Sorry, we have very few Schoenberg scores. You could try the University of California, Los Angeles. Schoenberg taught there for several years and has a hall named after him."

"Many thanks," said Tosca.

Back home, she set up her laptop, clicked on the Internet icon and typed UCLA in the Google search box. Navigating her way through the website, she studied several links before finding the UCLA university archives pages. She clicked on its list of collections and finally found a page with a phone number to call for reference. This is worse than following a string of clues in a murder, she thought as she dialed the number.

In answer to her questions a cheery voice told her to get back on the Internet and find the music library's special collections page. There'd be a phone number she could call to set up an appointment to view the Schoenberg scores. Tosca found the number, called and left a message. After an hour had passed and no return call came, Tosca decided she could bear to wait no longer. She retrieved the folder marked UCLA and studied the Mapquest driving directions to the university. She never used the GPS while behind the wheel, finding it too distracting. Instead, she always wrote the directions down in large black marker letters that could easily be read with a quick glance.

Her research meant a trek to Los Angeles of at least an hour and possibly double that time to drive back to Orange County during the late afternoon rush hour if her investigation of Schoenberg's archives was lengthy. Well, nothing for it but to get on the road.

As she drove she listened to a CD of Schoenberg's opera, *Moses und Aron.* She recalled a critic's harsh opinion of the composer, calling him "the scary twelve-tone inventor who killed harmony and nearly all else that the conventional concert-goer expects." How unjust, she thought as the frenzied music soared through the car's six speakers.

Tosca repeated the number twelve aloud. Her research showed that some scholars believed Schoenberg cared more about numbers than sound, mixing them up to create a new row of notes that could be played backwards. Weird, she thought, but understandable for the musician who was said to have found that all existing music of the time was boring.

She also discovered that composer Charles Ives hung melodies he composed on the wall for two months to see if he liked them and marked the notes with numbers for future reference. Was that what Schoenberg did? But why did the professor pick out those two particular bars of music and hang them up? She was probably chasing the wrong rainbow.

The route took her north on the 405 freeway, which she exited at Sunset Boulevard, a magical landmark to Tosca because it was featured in the classic Gloria Swanson movie of the same name. The street fascinated every Brit who longed to drive along the curvy, tree-lined historic road, hoping for a peek at the homes of famous stars.

The entrance to UCLA was unexpected and almost hidden. Only a small wooden sign indicated the presence of one of the largest university complexes on the West Coast. Among the residences, halls, museums, institutes, gardens, libraries, a stadium, a theater and dozens of other structures, Tosca soon found Schoenberg Hall but discovered that its only connection to the composer was his name on the building. His archives, she was told, were housed several miles away at the University of Southern California. So much for diligent Internet research. I should have waited for the return phone call, she thought, and saved time.

Given directions, she retraced part of her trip and arrived at the USC campus. Unlike UCLA, it was located far from the glamour of Hollywood, although the setting was park-like with grassy areas, tree-lined walkways, fountains, courtyards and a sculpture garden. Some of the buildings were in the Italian Romanesque style, while the Schoenberg archives were housed in a modern, two-story institute named for the composer. She was directed to the music building, where she asked at the information desk to talk to someone about Arnold Schoenberg. A forty-something woman appeared from a rear office, and introduced herself to Tosca.

"How can I help you?"

From her purse Tosca once more brought out her copy of the music fragment on Whittaker's wall.

"Do you know what these numbers mean? This is part of a score composed by Arnold Schoenberg."

"I'm sorry, I'm not a specialist on him, and there's no one here to help you right now. Can you come back tomorrow?"

"I've driven up from Orange County, but, yes, I could come back. Can you tell me anything personal about Schoenberg?"

"It's common knowledge among his followers that he loved numbers. He says he dreamed in numbers, though we don't know exactly what he meant."

"Isn't there any explanation?"

"Well, mathematics and music are interrelated, of course, but how this particular composer connected the numbers and notes, I can't say." She studied the bar of music more closely. "You know, Schoenberg didn't use the twelve-tone scale until late in his career, and I've never come across his scores with numbers added. I'm sorry. I'm not the person who can help you. Call tomorrow any time after ten a.m. and ask for Carol Dane." She wrote the extension number on a sheet of paper and handed it to Tosca.

In the car once more, Tosca reviewed the directions back to Newport Beach, checked the map she kept open on the passenger seat and found her way onto the 405 South. Irritated at the time wasted, she failed to notice the flashing lights in her rearview mirror until she'd driven a mile down the freeway with the California Highway Patrol motorcycle cop close behind. She pulled over onto the shoulder and stopped. When approached, she put down her window.

"Superintendent, or is it Detective Sergeant? I am so, so glad you are here! Talk about serendipity. I am totally lost. Imagine your showing up just when I need your help.

The problem is, your wonderful freeways are much more complicated than England's. Of course, your entire country is probably better, especially your history, which is so much more vigorous than ours." She picked up the map from the passenger seat and showed it to the officer. "Can you point out exactly where I am? I'd be extremely appreciative. I've read all about how helpful the California highway patrol is to visitors from abroad like me. Of course, I've watched the television program *CHiPs.* Did you have a part? You look like you'd fit perfectly. Now, can you help me?"

Appearing flummoxed, the officer explained where she was. He told her to please slow down and she was lucky not to get a ticket, only a warning this time. She thanked him profusely, promised to send some mead to the highway patrol headquarters and went on her way.

In Newport Beach she stopped in at the public library and checked out two more books on Arnold Schoenberg. Perhaps she'd find the answer she sought within their pages.

The next morning, after waiting impatiently for ten o'clock , Tosca called USC to make an appointment to view the Schoenberg archives. Four minutes later she was pacing around the cottage's small living room, waving her arms.

"*Kawgh ki!* Damn! Transferred to Vienna! Double *kawgh ki!* I can't go to Vienna!" She let out a stream of piercing high-C notes.

J.J. came dashing down from her rooftop sunbathing session. "What on earth's the matter? Were you swearing in Cornish again?"

"My best clue. Swiped. Hijacked to Austria."

"Calm down, Mother. Tell me in whole sentences what you mean."

Tosca related the conversation she'd had with the librarian at USC. "The Schoenberg family successfully sued USC for his archives to be taken back to his birthplace, Vienna. They've gone! Gone!"

"Well, that makes sense to me," said J.J. "Obviously the court agreed with the family. They should indeed be given custody of them."

"Oh, you're no help. How can I complete my research? USC even renamed the Schoenberg building. It's now the Bing Theater. Bing! That pipsqueak Crosby, I suppose. Well, time for tea."

As she picked up the canister containing loose Darjeeling tea leaves, she wondered how that amateur geologist with The Hat was getting on with his FBI friend.

TWENTY

Thatch's phone rang.

"Okay, buddy. You owe me another lunch." Delano's voice sounded upbeat.

"Dan! Don't tell me you got results from that rock already?"

"I sure have. Had to pull a few strings, but it was a slam dunk, the Quantico lab tells me. Want to meet at Shaunessey's tomorrow?"

"It's only ten o'clock right now. How about in a couple of hours today?" The chuckle Thatch heard from the other end of the line and Delano agreeing to a noon meeting sent him running upstairs to shower, shave and change into a clean shirt and jeans.

As he drove toward the restaurant Thatch pondered Delano's "slam dunk" comment. What did it mean? If the talon-like nodules in the rock were indeed fingertips, then the lab could determine the DNA. The Israelis, he recalled, had recently developed an improved technique for extracting genetic material from fossils, including human bones. Certainly the Quantico lab would be up to date on the process. On the other hand, DNA depended upon good quality and uncontaminated samples. The DNA chain must be intact with the strands not fragmented.

Would Thatch's own theory about the make-up of the rock itself prove correct? He hoped Dan's report would be able to tell him the exact composition of the rock, when it was created and the age of its contents.

Seated once more at the same table and with Stiegl beers in front of them, the two leaned toward each other.

"Right," said Delano. "Let's cut to the chase. The bottom line is, the forensic anthropologist in our lab confirms that your find is human. Belonged to a young person, maybe late teens, early twenties. The scan shows a skeletal hand that was severed just above the wrist. It was encased in cement."

Thatch nodded. "Yes, that's what I figured, too."

"As you also figured, I'm sure," Delano went on, "the rock began to deteriorate, not only because of the ocean environment but also because the cement mixture was pretty loose. There was too much water in the mix when it was formed, plus whoever made it forgot or didn't know enough to add some fine gravel to the concrete. So it deteriorated faster than intended."

"The sea air, I suppose, but isn't concrete gray?" said Thatch.

"You can buy white cement. It's more expensive, but that's what your guy did, and he added a pale pink pigment to make the rock look more natural."

"Was there any skin or flesh clinging to the bones inside the rock?"

"No. We'd thought that the part of the hand still inside the rock might be mummified, because cement is fairly porous after it dries, at least at a microscopic level. This would allow the moisture in the tissues to soak into the cement and dry out the hand. But in this case the hand has decayed, leaving only the bones."

"Does that mean you have DNA?" said Thatch.

"Yes, we do. I've made a copy of the reports for you, but I'm going to have to pass this along to the Newport Beach Police Department." Delano took a brown envelope from his briefcase and handed it to Thatch.

"Dan, you've made my day. I'm relieved it's worked out. There's a very special lady on Isabel Island who'll want to know she can stop worrying and leave everything to the local cops."

"Isn't your son a police officer there?"

"Yes, Andrew's a bicycle patrolman on the island. He'll be interested in this, too, of course, because he'd kind of dismissed Tosca's suspicions."

"Tosca? Is that someone's name or a place in Italy?" said Delano, laughing.

"I know, I know. Her mom was an opera fan, and she named her children after characters from various operas. I looked up the story of *Tosca*, and the heroine is one very fiery, passionate beauty."

"Does the lady on the island match that description?" asked Delano.

"The beauty part, yes, and she's sure passionate about trying to solve what she believes is a murder. Fiery? Questionable. She got pretty upset when I asked for ice in my drink."

"Must be a Brit, right?"

MacAulay nodded. "To the core. Worse, she's Cornish."

"Meaning?"

"Not really sure yet, but different from your average English person."

The two men grinned at each other and, after ordering lunch, turned their talk to Delano's family. After filling MacAulay in on his son's upcoming medical school graduation and his wife's new car, Delano looked at his friend, hesitated, then asked, "How's Christine?"

MacAulay didn't reply for a few moments. Finally, he said, "No change."

The brevity of the statement discouraged further discussion, and Delano took the hint. Thatch was grateful for Dan's understanding. He knew he shouldn't be ashamed of the situation with Christine, but he'd been in denial for so long it had taken an effort to accept it. The men moved on to discussing the upcoming baseball season and golf until they left the restaurant.

"We've struck pay dirt, Tosca. Call me back. "

Thatch's triumphant message left on her iPhone gave Tosca pause. Had this man with the broken nose solved the crime? *A-barth am Jowl!* Damn! This was her case, not his. She'd found the fingers in the rock. She'd talked to the neighbors. She'd tackled the professor in his den. She'd discovered a possible clue. And to top it all off, she'd driven all over those frightening eight-lane freeways to research Schoenberg and his music. Okay, it was true that Thatch was getting the rock tested, but that was his sole contribution so far.

"How dare he solve this without me," she said to J.J. as her daughter prepared to bake salmon fillets for them both. "*Gast! Kawgh ki!* I'm as mad as a boiled owl."

"Mother, stop swearing. He probably hasn't solved it. Calm down. There you go again, jumping to conclusions. Why don't you hear what he has to say before you get so upset? And watch that knife."

"I am not upset," said Tosca, scattering red peppers over the counter and onto the floor as the pace of her chopping increased. "I am merely saying that if Thatch is going to interfere, then …"

"What? You'll force-feed him that godawful mead?" J.J. and Tosca laughed as the tension lifted. "You and Thatch make a good team, and he seems to have amazingly great contacts in law enforcement. You couldn't ask for a better buddy."

"Buddy? Really, J.J., your language is truly going downhill. Too much hanging around those race car drivers. Still, I must admit they are a lot of fun, especially the NASCAR types. I'm amazed it's such a big business here. You'd never see that in England, of course."

"No, you certainly wouldn't. Instead, the UK glories in its violent soccer hooligans."

"Yes, I have to admit you're right. As a matter of fact, I'm tossing most of my preconceived ideas about

America out the window. Anyway, let's have dinner, then I'll return Thatch's call."

An hour later Tosca took her phone out of her purse, mounted the spiral staircase to the roof deck and dialed. He answered his phone before it finished ringing its first few notes.

"Hi, Tosca. I assume you got my message. I have some very interesting news for you. How about a drink down your way if it's not too late?"

"Yes, Thatch, that would be very nice." Tosca kept her voice deliberately soft and quiet. No sense letting him know she was *serrys,* though most of her annoyance had already dissipated. "I'll meet you at the ferry. There's a bar on the peninsula that intrigues me. How about eight o'clock?"

"Great," said Thatch.

If he noticed the coolness in her tone, he didn't remark on it. Probably too excited about his great find, whatever it was, or maybe, Tosca reflected, his hearing was off. She hadn't observed any cauliflower ear or similar deformity, but he looked like he'd hold his own in the boxing ring. He seemed the type to have been in plenty of scrapes in his lifetime and always come out the victor. Ha! Not this time. I'm going to take charge here, she decided, and let him know just whose criminal case this is.

Thatch arrived at the ferry all smiles. "Where's this mysterious bar you've picked out? I can't think of a single one over there that would be suitable for you. Are you sure you don't want to go to the Ritz in Newport Center?"

Tosca said nothing, smiled politely and allowed him to pay the fare. After disembarking, she led the way just one block from the dock and stood outside The Dirty Dozen Saloon, which occupied the corner lot. Loud rock music poured through its doors. The windows were fogged with smoke, and two of the panes were broken.

Thatch laughed. "This is it? One of my favorites, but are you sure you want to go inside?"

"Of course. I like these kinds of bars. Back home I found some of my best gossip at a grungy pub like this near Buckingham Palace. It was frequented by many of the queen's kitchen staff. Don't forget I'm supposed to be writing my impressions of America for my new column, and this is one of the perfect places to observe Americans at play. Mind if we sit at the bar?"

They took seats on torn, vinyl-covered stools at the long, scarred wooden bar and ordered beers, a half pint of bitter for Tosca and a Lone Star for Thatch.

He turned to her and said, "Okay, here's the skinny. Dan Delano confirms your theory. The bones are human, probably a young man or woman. Could be one of Orange County's missing students. One or two disappear every year."

"Do you think the bones could be tied in to the other case, the killing of the ferry boat kid?" said Tosca.

"Who knows? But please, stay out of it. The Newport police are going to reopen their missing persons cold case files, so now we can relax. No more sleuthing, Tosca."

Seated at one of the Newport Beach Library's microfiche machines with a stack of boxes holding rolls of film at her elbow, Tosca studied the *Orange County Register* files dated five and six years earlier. As she scrolled, Thatch's words still rankled. No more sleuthing, indeed. Cheeky devil.

Halting the microfilm frequently to read various headlines, and surprised to see so much international reporting while appreciating the newspaper's worldwide coverage, Tosca grudgingly admitted to herself that American journalists weren't so bad after all.

They could certainly write, and while the spelling annoyed her, she admired the factual approach they brought to their stories. Though I don't think much of the tabloids here, she muttered. Not a single full frontal. That *National Enquirer* is a pallid echo of the British scandal sheets. Ours are far more salacious and insulting. We can make a recipe for pea soup sound porno-sexy.

Following the train of thought, Tosca's mind inevitably strayed to the reason for her banishment to "the colonies." The image of what she had discovered at the palace refused to leave her mind until she forced her eyes back to the monitor in front of her. As she read, she began whistling, her signal to herself to stop dwelling on the past.

An outraged hiss from the person at the next machine brought Tosca's lips together in a straight line. She whispered "Sorry," and continued to scroll through the film. She stopped the wheel at one point to peer closer to the screen to read the article, a short piece on a missing Asian student. She pressed the print button and then kept going, searching for the names of other missing students over the past several years.

By the end of three hours she had printed out copies of reports of six missing students in the area who had disappeared during the time frame in which she was interested. Stiff from sitting so long, Tosca stretched, gathered up the pile of printouts, paid for them at the information desk and walked down the short hill to a café to order coffee.

While she waited she decided to call Thatch, unable to resist sharing her news. At his mumbled "Hello?" she said, "Oh, did I catch you at a bad time?"

"No. I'm pleased to hear from you. What's going on?"

"Guess what I've found? A treasure trove of missing people. Oh, don't be so cranky. I do feel sorry for them. It's really and truly sad, but there's still this awful Professor Whittaker walking around. I am positive he killed one of them and cut off his or her hands."

"Tosca, you are unbelievably impulsive. How can you shoot from the hip like that? There are all kinds of scenarios to explain the rock. Don't move. I'm coming over."

She grinned. Guess that's one way to get attention from a special chap, she reflected, and this one is very, very special. Could be a keeper.

"I'm at the coffee shop down the hill from the library," she said.

"Be there in five."

What delicious phrases Americans come up with, she thought. Brief. Decisive. We do seem to stretch things out back home with excessive politeness and unnecessary words. "Be there in five." How explicit. If it were me, I would have replied, "The coffee shop? How very nice of you to suggest getting together. It's a perfect place to meet. I do believe I can be there in, let's say, five minutes or as close as possible to that time. Does that suit you? Are you quite sure? Not too late?"

When she saw Thatch striding through the door, she felt a rush, a thrill, and waved a tiny lace-edged handkerchief. She waited for his reaction, but he ignored the fanciful gesture and sat down opposite her. She figured that, despite his displeasure at her interference with criminal matters, he was intrigued with the crime. Maybe that geology stuff is getting boring for him, she thought. Perhaps he even regrets retiring. She showed him the newspaper articles of the missing persons she'd printed out at the library.

"Three were Asians studying science at UCI," she said. "Two were from China and one from Korea. The fourth missing person was Persian, studying jazz at Saddleback College, but he's really Iranian since it's all one country."

"Never let the Persians hear you say that," interjected Thatch, "but go on."

"The sixth was from Eugene, Oregon." Tosca sat back in the booth, grinning.

Thatch acknowledged her words with a nod and said, "I suppose this sixth student, Paul Holloway, was studying piano and composition with Professor Haiden Whittaker, right?"

"*Mal!* You've been talking to your son."

Thatch laughed. "I guess that's Cornish for damn. Well, yes, Andy's keen on delving into cold cases, which this one was until you shook things up. But I told you, it's a police matter now."

"Tell me more. Fill me in. Can I see the Holloway file?"

"Of course not, but I can tell you this. A thorough investigation at the time turned up zip on Holloway. Several students, friends and his landlord were questioned, but the police hit a dead end, if you'll forgive the pun. The professor was just back from attending a music event at the Grosses Festspielhaus in Salzburg, Austria, where, incidentally, my favorite beer is brewed. The cops talked to him, and he said he had no idea what might have happened to his student. So he's not a suspect. He's highly regarded, you know."

"I hear you can buy bottles of brandy in Salzburg with Mozart's face on the label," said Tosca. "Do you think if they did that with Beethoven's face on a whiskey bottle, it could be called Beethoven's Fifth?"

Thatch laughed. "That joke's so old it has gray hair." He quickly became serious, going on to describe how the police had tried to contact the youth's only relative, the grandfather who had raised him.

"Unfortunately, Paul's grandfather died a year earlier. Seems they were poor farm people, but the kid was incredibly talented. Neighbors said he was a child prodigy. Tall and broad shouldered, he had huge hands that could stretch over nine keys on the piano, according to his fellow students. Not the kind of guy I myself would expect to be a musician. Did you know this interesting trivia, that Russian peasants were excellent violinists because of their strong, muscular hands? I had a girlfriend in college who told me that. She was a music student."

"So Paul, the farmer's son, put his strong hands to good use on the piano," Tosca said.

"We also know," Thatch continued, "that Holloway was the professor's favorite because of his talent, and Whittaker gave him private lessons at his home. They both shared a passion for Arnold Schoenberg."

"I wonder why Holloway didn't study at The Juilliard School in New York? Surely he would have won a scholarship there," said Tosca.

"Refused to leave the West Coast, we're told. His granddad was in bad health, and the kid didn't want to be clear across the country if something happened."

"Schoenberg," mused Tosca. "There's that bar of Schoenberg music that Whittaker had on his wall. As soon as I left I saw him taking it down, I think I told you that. I'm positive it has significance, seeing that both the teacher and the student were admirers of the composer. Are you a musician, too?" She lifted his right hand and studied the calluses. "Are these from picking a guitar?"

"A ukulele."

"So you do have a musical bent."

"No, not really," he said. "I can only play a three-note scale. My buddy in Dana Point, Dick Ribble, has been trying to teach me for years, and he's great on the uke, but I guess I just don't have the talent. He kept telling me it only took three minutes to learn, but we were laughing at my efforts so much, I didn't get far."

"Well, I definitely think Schoenberg plays a role here. I am positive there's a connection, some kind of code in that piece of music."

"Uh oh, I'm beginning to recognize that smug smile of yours. What?"

Tosca explained how she'd written the notes and numbers down, as far as she could remember them. "The numbers were easy to recall, but to make sure I copied down the musical notes correctly, I still need to find the original score."

They parted, Thatch dropping Tosca off on Isabel Island after telling her he had some business to attend to. The mysterious Christine, she wondered? Who was this woman?

Back home, Tosca rummaged through her by-now burgeoning files of research. She'd been living in America only a few weeks, she realized, and was already investigating a murder, or perhaps two. She was convinced there was a body belonging to the hand somewhere, so it was fair game to pursue the murderer—who, she just knew, was the professor. As for the ferry boat killing, she'd get to that all in good time. She felt a personal interest in both murders because she'd found two of the most important clues, the rock and the silver aegina. Solving either crime could be her ticket home.

The next day, an hour after J.J. left on a four-day trip to Ohio for her next car race, the land phone in the kitchen rang. Still puzzling over the sheet music, Tosca picked up the receiver and spoke into it.

"Trevant residence. This is the female butler speaking."

Thatch's laugh from the other end of the line made her smile.

"Doesn't that make you the housekeeper?" he said.

"Of course not. Totally different duties."

"I'll never know, that's for sure. May I come over again? I just thought of something else."

"Yes, please do." She decided not to ask about his family emergency or who Christine was, despite her intense curiosity.

"See you in ten," he told her. "Oh, and I'll bring some beer, if that's all right. You won't need to break out the mead."

"I'm ready to make up another batch. It has to ferment for three months, you know."

"I hope to be deep in the Antarctic by then."

"Coward."

Thatch arrived and suggested they go out for lunch. They decided on an Italian restaurant but found it filled with tourists.

"There are no tables here, Tosca. Looks like a ferry ride is in order," he said. "How about we try Ruby's on the pier?"

She nodded, and they walked along the seafront boardwalk, then down the short gangplank to join others waiting for the incoming boat. After it docked and disgorged bicyclists, skateboarders, a crush of people and cars, Tosca and Thatch boarded. They sat on one of the narrow, weathered benches that ran the length of the ferry. Three vehicles trundled over the boat's wide planks as the attendant directed them forward and reminded the drivers to turn off their engines. The ferry was backed away from the dock. Thatch took two dollars and paid the attendant. After the brief trip across the channel, the pilot pulled in and docked on the peninsula.

"It's just a couple of blocks to the pier," Thatch told Tosca.

"My dear man, I have already been there several times. The pier is, of course, much shorter than most of ours in England," said Tosca, "but it suffices."

"Suffices?"

Tosca giggled. "Sorry, I know I can sound a bit pompous."

Ruby's, a 1950s-style diner famous for its hamburgers, was situated at the end of the Isabel Island pier. Fishermen leaned over the rails, their poles and drop lines extended into the ocean thirty feet below, hoping to hook mackerel, halibut or sand bass.

Settling into a booth and thanking a waiter for bringing coffee, Tosca leaned toward Thatch expectantly.

"What did your FBI friend tell you?" she said. "Did the lab finish its report? Who's the victim, Whittaker's wife? The student? What was the murder method?"

Thatch stretched his legs under the table and smiled at her. "Do you ever ask one question at a time?" he said.

"You're making small talk while there's a murderer walking around?"

"Man, I never knew the Brits were prone to such exaggeration. All right, Tosca, I have more details about what I told you before when you insisted on going to that sleazy bar. The FBI confirms that the piece of rock you gave me contains the left hand of a person who died around five years ago. The X-rays show that the fingers are still attached to a good portion of the palm and wrist."

"I knew it," said Tosca triumphantly, "but how on earth did his fingers get stuck inside a rock?"

"Remember I told you about the sandstones in the desert? Dan says the FBI confirms what I suspected, but I wanted to be sure before telling you. Didn't want you to go charging off in all directions." He smiled to soften the words.

"How considerate of you. Now please, tell me more."

"It's not a real rock. It's a fake. Someone made it and most likely the other one you saw. They are made from cement and mixed with different colored pigments during various stages of hardening to resemble sandstone. That's why I was suspicious."

"Yes, I remember now. You told me that sandstone is formed from layers of ancient sand."

"Right, the kind you find in parts of Death Valley. It takes centuries to erode, unlike the rock from the professor's yard."

"Death Valley?" she asked. "That's the California desert, isn't it?"

"Yes, but sandstone is mostly found in Anza-Borrego State Park east of San Diego. There are concretions that look like cannonballs, so they wouldn't have been difficult to simulate. I imagine the hand was completely encased, but then the cement crumbled away, exposing the fingertips."

"How ingenious."

He watched Tosca's blue eyes suddenly come alive with excitement.

"Thatch, let's dig up Professor Whittaker's garden and find the rest of the body." She stood up abruptly.

"Uh, it doesn't work like that here. You claimed you found this outside his yard on the sidewalk, so anyone could have put it there. The cops would have no cause to question him." He watched her blush as she fumbled for words.

"What if I saw it roll out from under his gate?" She sat down again.

"Did you?"

"He grows poppies and hollyhocks in all the wrong places."

Thatch was silent for a moment. "Did you see this rock outside of his yard?" His tone was firmer.

"His voice got really squeaky when I put him under pressure."

"Tosca, as far as you are concerned, Professor Whittaker is out of the picture. The police will take it from here. More coffee?" he asked, looking around for their waiter.

"No, thank you. I want to hear more about what your FBI friend told you."

Thatch related a few more of Delano's findings, adding, "The sandstones could have been brought here from anywhere. Mexico, maybe."

"You're giving me pretty sketchy information," said Tosca, "but then, this isn't Scotland Yard. Yes, yes, I concede that Americans are marvelous detectives," she added hastily at Thatch's expression, "and your technology is said to be flawless, but let's face it, the Australians are way ahead of anyone else electronically."

Wryly acknowledging she was right, although he knew U.S. law enforcement agencies had far more advanced intel equipment and programs than the general public realized, Thatch shrugged and said nothing.

"Sorry," said Tosca. "I take that back. Please forgive my rudeness. I want to hear more details of the lab report."

"Sure you're ready? Some of it's pretty gruesome."

"If I'm to be a crime reporter I'd better get used to the nether underpinnings of the criminal mind."

"Tosca, there you go again. Nether underpinnings? What's that, a Victorian petticoat?"

"Could be," she replied, smiling.

"Okay. Well, Dan said that figuring out which species bones are from is sometimes a puzzle because some animal bones, like a bear's front claws, are similar to those of a human hand. Bones have bumps, ridges and various other characteristics depending on their function in the body and on which species that body belongs to. But DNA solves all that."

As he spoke Tosca took out a small notebook and pen from her purse and began writing down his words. "So what's the age of the bones? You said they were from a young person."

"Most forensic anthropologists can only take a stab at age unless the bones are from a child," Thatch continued, "because of their predictable growth pattern. Baby teeth, for instance, and ribs where they join the breastbone. These are smooth in young children but become pitted and sharp as we age."

"Good heavens! You mean to tell me I've been walking around with dents in my ribs for years?" Tosca prodded her ribcage. "Who told you all this, your friend Dan?"

"It's in the report and backed up by one of the top scientists in the field."

"All right. Go on, is there more?"

Thatch took her through the forensic process that determines stature. "How thick the bones are is a clue, and as for the person's sex, the lower bone on the side of the thumb, called the radius, can be helpful in distinguishing between male and female."

"And we have that bone, don't we?" said Tosca.

"The hand you found was cut off an inch above the wrist, so we have a good partial."

"You said 'person.' Why can't they tell if it was a male or a female?"

"They probably do know, but they didn't tell me."

"Was the lab able to estimate a time of death?"

"They figure five years. Come on, Tosca, that's enough, isn't it?"

"Just one more extremely crucial question, then I'll buy you an ice cream. How did he die?"

Thatch shook his head. "You're relentless. I have no idea,"

"If we find the other parts of him, would there be any dried blood clinging to the bones?" she said.

"I see your tabloid imagination at work. Blood? Doubtful. Depends where the other parts are buried. If there was moisture around, the corpse would decay due to the bacteria that causes putrefaction in warm, moist environments." He paused at Tosca's expression of intense concentration.

"What if it was dry?" she said.

"Look, Tosca, you're thinking like a forensic pathologist, granted, but this entire matter is in the hands of the police. We're out of it. Leave it to the experts. Hey, enough talk of death. Let's get that ice cream."

They took the ferry back across the bay and walked over to the ice cream stand on the island's main street. As Tosca was paying, Thatch's phone rang.

"Andy? Hi, son." He paused to listen, standing stock still, then said, "When did Christine leave? I'll be right there."

He turned to Tosca. "I'm so sorry. Another emergency. I need to take you home."

"No problem. I understand. I hope it's not too serious."

Thatch didn't respond and they walked quickly to his car, where he bade her goodbye.

TWENTY-ONE

Thatch drove well over the posted speed limit, weaving expertly in and out of traffic as he headed toward the seaside town of San Clemente, not caring if he was pulled over by the highway patrol. Andy's message had set his heart racing despite the discipline drummed into him during his training as a member of the Secret Service and the many years learning how to remain calm. Because of Christine, his twenty-eight year old daughter, he had come to recognize that personal emergencies demanded far more self-control than those in his former profession, more than he ever imagined existed.

For a long time, ever since the diagnosis, he had deceived himself into believing her condition was curable, that the disease would burn itself out, and she'd be her kind, intelligent, beautiful self again. In the beginning, month after month, he had scoured the country, seeking yet another doctor or chasing a new cure. But after three years of frustration, Thatch had accepted the reality of the paranoid schizophrenia that had first afflicted his daughter in her senior year at college, just months after her mother died. His heartache became a permanent part of his life.

Thatch talked to Christine daily on the phone he'd bought her, which she kept on her bedside table at the group home in which she lived. Once a college tennis champion and an A-student with her future brimming with promise, his daughter now languished in a semi-dark world where hallucinations, fortunately less frequent these days, could make her frantic with worry until she called him and he calmed her down with reassuring, soothing words.

"We're giving Christine a new medication. It's quite a break-through," her doctor had told Thatch two years earlier. The drug quelled much of the paranoia that accompanied her schizophrenia, but the occasional delusion still appeared without warning. She'd call him in a panic, and he'd drop everything to remind her she was simply having a hallucination. He'd talk her through the episode until she could think rationally again.

Thatch was always truthful with her, never flinching from calling the disease by name and telling her what she was hearing at that moment was her mind playing tricks on her.

"But I heard it on the wall," she'd say. "There's a microphone in there."

"Honey, run your fingers over the wall. You'll see there is no microphone or camera."

He was relieved that she usually listened to him. Her panic would subside, and she'd end up agreeing she was simply having a hallucination, that the CIA wasn't after her. In the space of minutes her spirits would change from depressed to upbeat. Thatch could tell by her voice when she was calm, and he'd thankfully finish the call.

This time, though, the situation was more serious. Andy's message said that Christine was convinced she was being evicted and had packed her belongings. She'd called Andy to come and get her. Thatch had no idea why she'd phoned her brother instead of him. When he drove up, he saw Andy waiting for him, sitting on the porch steps.

"She's gone."

Andy's anguished words hit Thatch like a hammer. "Why didn't you say so on the phone?"

"Didn't want you to kill yourself getting here, Dad, but I bet you drove like crazy anyhow."

Thatch put his arm around Andy's drooping shoulders and rang the bell of the ornate house where Christine lived with five other patients. A typical Craftsman built in the early 1930s, it sat well back from the quiet residential street, providing privacy behind its stand of ancient live oak trees in the front yard.

Jane Holliday, the supervisor, answered the door and ushered them in. 'I'm so sorry, Mr. MacAulay. She's never done this before. We thought she'd just gone out to the corner store. We had no reason to think this time was any different. She didn't say anything to anyone, and we didn't actually see her leave. She just called out to us in the office before she left. She's been doing so well lately."

Considered trustworthy patients, the six women residents had freedom to shop in the nearby stores, take walks on their own and live as normally as possible despite their disease. They were considered low risk as long as they took their medications every morning and evening, when the nurse dispensed the drugs, and attended the weekly counseling sessions.

Every now and then one or two of the patients would be offered the opportunity to work at a non-stressful job, such as sorting clothes at the Goodwill store. Inevitably, though, after a week or so, they would find it difficult to concentrate. Christine had tried five different jobs, but her lack of focus and recurring hallucinations forced her to quit. The longest she'd held a job was three weeks.

"When did she leave the house?" asked Thatch. They'd walked out to the front gate, anxiously looking up and down the street,

"Melanie said Christine went out just after lunch," said Mrs. Holliday. "She did see her carrying a small suitcase, but we have another patient here who never goes out without her backpack, so Melanie thought maybe Christine just wanted to have the suitcase with her."

The social worker told Andy and Thatch that when Christine failed to return for supper, two nurses had driven around the neighborhood, checking out nearby yards and houses on foot. No one had noticed a young woman with a suitcase.

"We started searching the nearby streets after Christine had been gone two hours, and we called the local grocery store," the supervisor told Thatch. "Then we called it in as a missing person to the police. They understand our situation and respond quickly."

As the supervisor finished talking, a sheriff's department car pulled up. Thatch, Andy and the supervisor watched as two deputies got out and approached. They nodded to Andy, and one approached Thatch.

"Hey, Thatch, real sorry to see you again under these circumstances. Don't worry, we'll find your daughter. We've already got two of our guys out there looking."

The group went inside the house and into the office. The supervisor told the remaining residents that the police wanted to ask a few questions, but after a few minutes it was plain the women had no information about Christine's plans or whereabouts.

Andy was asked, "When she called you to come pick her up, how did she sound?"

"Same as always, not excited or anything. I figured I'd come over and talk, just talk, and explain to her, as Dad and I both have over the years, that this is her home and she needs to stay here. I told her I'd be right over since it's my day off."

"Any case you're working on that would connect to your sister?"

"No, sir. Nothing."

"How about you, Thatch? I know you're retired, but could one of your old incidents have caught up with you? Some jerk you might have stopped getting too close to the president?"

At the suggestion, Thatch grew cold. There had been so many attempts. But since the assassination of John F. Kennedy, none had succeeded over his several years of guarding presidents Carter, Clinton and the two Bushes. No assassin had got past the Secret Service and succeeded, although John Hinckley had almost killed President Ronald Reagan.

"No. No one comes to mind. Not from the political arena anyway."

As he and Andy talked further, they heard the front door open and close. Both men spun around quickly. Thatch watched his daughter come into the hallway, followed by two deputies. He rushed to greet her. Christine was about to walk upstairs, her suitcase in hand. Thatch knew enough not to give in to the urge to grab her or yell at her for frightening them. Instead, he acted as if it were perfectly normal for her to be there and have a suitcase with her.

"Hi, darlin'. Were you going somewhere?" His voice was low and steady.

"Oh. Hi, Dad. Hi, Andy." She put the suitcase down. "I was told by the voices in the wall that I needed to take the train to San Diego, but I waited ages at the station, and it didn't come. These policemen gave me a ride back. I'll just put my suitcase away, then come down and talk to you both." Christine picked up the suitcase and went upstairs.

One of the cops said, "When we first checked the train station we didn't see any sign of her, so we kept going. When we circled back later, there she was on the platform."

"I can't thank you enough," said Thatch. "She's never run away from here before. Guess we need to keep closer tabs on her in future."

TWENTY-TWO

Tosca, concerned, called Thatch that evening. "Is everything all right? I was a little worried when you had to dash off like that," she said.

"Yes, everything's fine now. I appreciate your asking. So how's the Schoenberg research?"

"I'm well and truly stumped," Tosca said. "I've read everything I can find on him. One article was really interesting about a percussionist called Jackie Bertone who said that percussion is an additive to music, like a frame around a work of art. Well, the professor framed this particular bar of music. Maybe it has a hidden rhythm that means something special. It's worth considering. Why else would he take it off the wall after I commented on it?"

"People do all kinds of things for no reason, Tosca."

"I don't suppose you'd like to come over for a glass of mead, would you?"

"Mead? Thanks, but I'll bring my own brew. Maybe we can come up with an answer while the police continue their investigation."

Tosca hung up the phone. She was attracted to Thatch, but he surely was an odd duck. She hadn't seen anyone else in Newport Beach wearing a cowboy hat. This was sailing country. Maybe Mr. MacAulay fancied himself another Dennis Weaver, who wore a Stetson playing the Marshall Sam McCloud character in a TV detective series set in New York. He stuck out like a sore thumb. Or perhaps Thatch fancied himself a private investigator now that he was retired. She knew many cops became security guards and joined private detective agencies. Well, that's what she herself was focused on, solving both crimes and getting promoted, so he'd better not interfere too much. The man obviously had excellent contacts with law enforcement, and she was truly appreciative of his help, but if she wanted to return to her London newsroom in a blaze of glory, Thatch would need to step aside.

"Good evening, Tosca. May I come in?" Thatch called out through the open top half of the Dutch door.

"Reach in and pull back the bolt," she said, smiling as she came toward him. She pointed to his package. "Six cans of beer?"

"My favorite. One for you?" At her refusal, Thatch opened the refrigerator door in the small kitchen and, taking one can from the pack, put the remaining five beers on a lower shelf. He opened the can, took a short drink and sat on the sofa.

"No, no, not there," said Tosca. "I've set everything out over here."

"Everything?"

"Look, it's obvious to me that Schoenberg, the professor and the finger bones in the rock are all connected, and now we have a clue with the framed music."

"That's pretty thin as far as solid evidence goes," said Thatch. "But," he added, eyes twinkling, "I'll humor you. Maybe I'll pick up a few more Cornish words."

"Humor me? Don't worry, I'll convince you yet. Come on, sit here."

Thatch settled himself at the marble and glass table and studied three small stacks of papers. All music scores, they were arranged by date indicated by a yellow stick-on note.

"I looked up Schoenberg's concordance of melodies," said Tosca, touching the pile to her left. "My particular melody, as I call it, the one on Whittaker's wall, is attached to fourteen songs. Maybe each of the titles is a clue, so that's this first pile. The second one represents his most acclaimed compositions, and the third stack is all the Schoenberg compositions written during the final year of his life."

"Why did you categorize them this way?"

"I've no idea," she shrugged, "but they all have notations on them. Perhaps we could follow along chronologically with his thought processes."

"You spent all day finding these? Not much here."

"I'll have you know that Schoenberg's legacy includes essays, lectures, poems, letters, philosophical musings and tons of other writings. It took me hours of research to find that out. He was extraordinarily prolific and wrote in German, English and even French, but I found nothing on numerology except these."

Thatch picked up a piece of paper. "What's this note about Frank Zappa? He's a rock guitarist, not a classical musician."

"Surprised? J.J. was, too. Zappa was a Schoenberg fan. Listen to some of his CDs. Your son probably has some. Another interesting fact I found out is that the brain responds to harmony. Schoenberg's harmonies were atonal, or disharmonious. I wonder if a sociopath who listened to that stuff a lot could become affected by it."

Thatch got up and took another can of beer from the refrigerator. While there he reached down to the floor and picked up Tosca's jug of mead. "More?"

"Yes, thank you."

She watched as he poured the liquid gently into her glass. His hands, she thought, could cup a football or a woman's full breast with equal sureness.

"I don't know about music turning someone into a sociopath," said Thatch, "but it can affect teenagers, especially if they're tripping out. As far as Whittaker is concerned, we need to stick to the facts. I don't see anything on these music scores that's going to help us, so let's run down the list of things that involve groups of numbers."

"All my hard work gone to waste? All right, let's hear your own brilliant theory."

"The most obvious is that they are phone numbers, maybe international numbers. Read them out to me again." He closed his eyes and prepared to listen.

"The first set of numbers," she said, reading from her notes, "is 3225718 followed by 11640666. I don't know any international dialing code that matches them. I call the UK all the time, and you have to dial 011 first for whatever country you're calling."

"I know. Despite all my travels abroad, I can't come up with any that resemble these either, but we can't discount the possibility that they are phone numbers. Maybe he threw in a couple of extra twos or sixes as a code. What else? They could be bank account numbers, but there aren't enough digits, and there are too many for a safety deposit box number. Maybe invoice numbers?"

"I vote for a countdown on the Doomsday Clock or a pattern for knitting socks."

"Don't get facetious, Tosca. This is serious business."

"Right." She sighed and drank more mead. "A birth date? Let me check when Schoenberg was born." She opened a bulging file folder. "September 13, 1874. So that's 9131874. No, that won't fit either. Damn. My eyes are sore. Let's take a break. How about banging out a tune on that banjo thing of yours?"

Thatch grinned. "It's called a ukulele, honey. I'll go get it."

He returned from his truck with the musical instrument and began to play. Soon he was singing, too. Tosca found she couldn't take her eyes off him, finding his complete absorption in the music giving her an unexpected thrill.

After ten minutes he set the ukulele down and said, "Let's get back to business."

"Maybe these are measurements," said Tosca, "like a certain number of paces forward, back and sideways. There was a Sherlock Holmes case like this. He paced off from an oak tree and found buried treasure."

"I doubt we are seeking buried treasure."

"You're right. More like another clue. Haiden's the type who likes to play games, judging by the Schoenberg score. So if it's another clue, maybe it tells where to find it, like an address. Something like 32757 Eighteenth Street and 116406 Sixty-Sixth Street?"

"An address?" He stared off into the distance, through the open door. "Read the numbers again. No, let me see them." He studied the sheet of paper. "Hey! When you read the numbers out you didn't tell me there was a period in the first set of numbers and a minus mark with the second. An address! Tosca! You're a genius. Of course that's it." Thatch jumped up and hugged her.

"Thatch, you're smothering me. So the numbers are an address? Then it must be in New York, though I didn't think house numbers ran that high in Manhattan."

"No, no, no, not a street address. Jeez, I'm such an idiot. How could I have missed it?"

"What is it then? You said that's it, and now it's not? You're driving me crazy. Hey, *skiansekigyon,* where are you going?"

Thatch ran through the front door, took the steps down three at a time and after a couple of minutes came bounding back. He was carrying a small device with a short, thick antenna.

"What was that you called me?" he said. "Anything like the Cornish word for idiot?"

His eyebrows raised when Tosca blushed as deeply as the first time they'd met.

"Never mind," she said, "but it wasn't rude. On the contrary. Tell me, what's that in your hand? Hope it's not some newfangled iPod. You've probably got a thousand country western songs on it. Are you going to answer my question?"

"This is a portable GPS unit. Global Positioning System. Runs on batteries."

"I know very well what a GPS is," said Tosca. "I have the application on my iPhone. Most cars are equipped with them to give directions to an address. Is this one different?"

"No, standard. In addition to maps, the unit shows latitude and longitude."

"Why do we need to know that?"

"Because that's what Whittaker's numbers represent, if I'm right. They're a precise address." He switched on the device and punched several keys. "Look, see these numbers? They're coordinates. They represent where we're standing right now. Here's your house, where that little arrow is pointing. Remember that movie, *Close Encounters of the Third Kind?* The military were given the coordinates of the mountain so they could meet the space ship. Using a globe, they traced the longitude from the South Pole westward across the U.S. until their fingers met to pinpoint a mountain called Devil's Tower in Wyoming. Today, they'd have used a GPS."

"Are you a movie buff?" said Tosca, amused.

"Don't change the subject. I'm punching in Whittaker's numbers. Let's see what the GPS comes up with. It'll tell us the exact location."

Tosca watched intently while Thatch pressed a button and entered the numbers. The small screen sprang to life, showing a map. He stared at it without speaking for several moments.

"Well? Don't just stand there. What's the address?" said Tosca.

"There isn't one."

"So it's not working? Ha! Out of batteries?"

"No, Tosca. It is working, but it's not a street address nor a city. It's a vast expanse of nothing, but a magical place. We call it Anza-Borrego. I know it well. We go there camping all the time. In fact, there's a Borrego Springs Resort, very popular spot. Its latitude is 33.25762, and the longitude is −116.40619. Can't think why I didn't catch on to this sooner. The area we want is farther south of the Springs, and it's all desert."

"Desert? Do you think that's where the professor hid his next clue? Where is this desert?"

"Southeast. About two and a half hours from here, not far from the Mexican border. It's huge."

He explained that it was one of his favorite haunts when he went off on his frequent trips to study geology. "I go there to read the rocks."

Thatch spoke enthusiastically about his hobby, the GPS unit forgotten, and Tosca was mesmerized as he described some of his most enjoyable discoveries in the area: the sandstone formations, the canyons and sand dunes left when the sea retreated millions of years earlier. He talked of the exposed cliffs showing their layers of life, marine and otherwise, after a series of earthquakes over the centuries. He described the masses of desert dune primroses and sand verbena.

"There are bighorn sheep, kit foxes, coyotes and…"

"Wait, wait," interrupted Tosca. "Don't tell me anymore. Let's go there right now. If the professor decided it was important enough to record that spot, then we need to find the reason."

"I wonder why he displayed the coordinates so prominently on his wall? Takes hubris to do that if it is related to Paul's disappearance," said Thatch.

"Doesn't surprise me in the least. That man's ego is as big as an elephant. I'm betting he never imagined anyone would recognize that small piece of Schoenberg's score after music students stopped coming to his house. Probably gave him immense satisfaction to have it in full view and believe that no one would figure it out. So let's follow it up."

"I'm not sure it's worth following up, Tosca. We should go digging in the desert? For what?"

"Look, if you don't want to go, I'll find it myself. It might be the answer to the whole situation."

Thatch shook his head and said, "All right, you've twisted my arm. You'd only get lost out there, so okay, I'll take you. I'm not sure about your clue. It seems far-fetched to me, but I know you'll love the desert. It's a very special place. "

"Wonderful. I'll get my jacket." She jumped up. "Come on! Stop lollygagging. Grab that hat of yours, and let's go."

"It's midnight," Thatch protested. He spoke so quietly that Tosca was stopped in her tracks.

"What? Oh. Really? How early can we leave tomorrow?"

TWENTY-THREE

Tosca was waiting on the sidewalk when Thatch arrived at eight o'clock. Agreeing to stop for breakfast somewhere along the way, they set out in his pickup. He wore his Hatillo summer straw Stetson and his oldest cowboy boots. Tosca, her slender figure accentuated by a tailored denim shirt and her only pair of jeans, sat almost on the edge of the passenger seat. In her hands she clutched the GPS unit. At her feet was her parasol.

On Interstate 5 they drove past the two remaining nuclear reactors of the San Onofre power plant. In the early 1990s, the story goes, two terrorists drove by the plant with cameras, snapping pictures as they passed. Both would be known worldwide in 2001 as 9/11 hijackers.

"Who owns this large ranch?" asked Tosca two minutes later, indicating the area to her left.

Thatch turned his head to grin at her. "The United States. It's a Marine base. Camp Pendleton."

"Well, pardon me, but I saw a buffalo under that oak tree."

Thatch laughed. "First, we call them bison, and I'm proud to say the noble animal you saw is the symbol on the flag of my home state of Wyoming. Second, a hundred-head herd is allowed to roam free on Pendleton's one hundred twenty-five thousand acres. Third, the camp is home to two dozen endangered birds and other species, and fourth, that's called a coastal oak, ma'am, not just an oak tree. Its acorns are poisonous."

"I shall be sure not to chew on any."

Within forty minutes Tosca and Thatch had turned off the freeway to head inland on State Highway 78 toward Escondido. The route took them into Ramona, a high desert, back country community where they stopped for a late breakfast in a rustic Western-style restaurant. Continuing on their way, they passed through Julian, a former mining town now famous for its apple orchards and fruit pies. After several more miles they came to a rural crossroads with a signpost that read S2A, pointing right, and S2 B, pointing left.

"That's the one we want, S2A. Turn right," said Tosca, reading from the GPS. Thatch swung the wheel, and soon the paved road gave way to a dirt trail.

"Are you sure this is correct? There's nothing out this way," said Tosca, straining to see ahead. Anza-Borrego, she decided, had none of the beauty of an English moor like Bodmin, although Bodmin's treacherous bogs can suck a cow under.

Here, she was faced with a vast emptiness that she speculated probably had its own brand of deceptively hidden danger. She'd read that illegal immigrants coming across the Mexican border often got lost and died of thirst beneath the gray summits of the softly folding mountains in the distance.

"I thought perhaps the professor might have had a summer cabin or something," said Tosca, "but judging by this godforsaken place, I suppose not. It's horribly desolate."

"Desolate? This?" Thatch smiled. "You are so wrong. The desert soil is filled with life, Tosca. Everywhere you look are habitats, holes in the ground that are home to white-footed mice, kangaroo rats, honey ants, scorpions, lizards and spiders, too many species to count."

"Shouldn't deserts have sand?"

"Yes, and we have lots of that, too," said Thatch. "The Algondones Dunes farther east rise to three hundred feet for miles and miles. They're home to albino grasshoppers and horned lizards."

"So you're a naturalist as well as a geologist?"

"No, not really. I like geology because it offers mysteries to solve, teasing us to figure out the history of our planet and how it was formed. I like to know who lived here thousands of years ago, what they hunted, the crops they grew, their lifestyle."

"It's bleak. Barren. How can you find it interesting?"

"I'll admit it's a bleak landscape in parts, but can't you feel the spirits of those who once were here?"

Tosca studied his face as he talked. "That's pretty poetic, Thatch. I didn't realize you're a romantic." This man's character has hidden depths, she thought, and so far, I like everyone.

"Guess I just like lonely places," he replied, "where you can sit in nature and forget everything else in your life except what's in front of your eyes." He stopped the car. "We must be close to our target. Maybe the professor came out here camping." He drove forward again after checking the GPS unit. "Or to get inspiration for his music. Don't laugh, Tosca, isn't that what composers do?"

"In this wilderness?" She gestured toward the horizon where nothing but dry arroyos and shale lay ahead.

"Why not? You should see it when the wildflowers are in bloom. There are areas where the landscape is carpeted with purple verbena, pink dune evening primrose, orange poppies and desert lilies. It's a spectacular sight. Besides, this isn't as harsh as the Mojave Desert or Death Valley, even though we're basically in the badlands."

"Sounds like you've been seeing too many Westerns."

"Nope. It's places like these that movie ideas come from. They're based on fact. The badlands are a fact, and you're in 'em, ma'am."

Tosca sat quietly. Suddenly, she called out, "Oh, look!"

"What?" Thatch slowed, glancing left and right.

"Lavender bushes! Fancy finding lavender here."

"Hey, why wouldn't lavender grow here? Man, I really thought you were on to something."

"All right, *skiansekigyon,* then what's that?" She pointed off to the left.

Thatch stepped on the brake and turned toward her. *"Skiansekigyon?* There's that word again. I'm not driving one more inch until you tell me what it means."

"It's a, uh, an expression."

"Of what, mental deficiency?"

"Endearment." Tosca blushed, holding her head low.

"You know," he said, easing off the brake and sending the truck into motion once more, "you could drive a guy crazy."

Tosca didn't reply. Instead, she pointed to several piles of gravel, asking what they were.

"That's a tailings plant, a gravel quarry." As they approached he added, "It looks abandoned. No equipment around, and the shack is boarded up."

"I know what a gravel quarry is, but in the middle of nowhere?"

"Cheaper to buy the raw material here on site. Saves on transportation charges. See those mountains? Companies buy one or a partial, then dynamite it. Machinery crushes and grinds the boulders into different sizes for building materials. Let's take a look."

He parked near several mounds of various-sized rocks, gravel and pebbles. One pile was covered with plant growth. They got out of the pickup and walked around, Tosca opening the parasol against the desert sun.

"I wonder if Whittaker hid a clue here, buried inside one of those mounds? Or what if we find a couple of arms with no hands instead of another clue?" She suppressed a shudder.

"You are the most bloodthirsty woman I have ever met." Thatch shook his head, smiling.

The remark increased her anxiety.

"Maybe this whole thing is a mistake," she said, eyeing the piles of gravel. "You did say the FBI lab definitely confirmed that there are fingers in that stone, didn't you?"

"Sounds like you're getting cold feet, Tosca. Don't worry. To answer your question, yes, Dan did confirm it, and no, it's not practical to bury body parts here. Although the site appears abandoned, it's pretty evident that people come and help themselves to a load or two of gravel to use in their driveways and landscaping."

He pointed at one of the mounds and continued talking. "Contractors take some, too, if the pieces are the right size. I'm surprised the original owners didn't clean the place out themselves when they closed it instead of leaving the stuff here. The piles probably reached more than twenty feet when the quarry was in operation. In any event this would be a poor place to hide something. People are coming and going all the time, and it's a little too close to Ocotillo, a little trailer community down the way."

They got back in the truck, Tosca closing the parasol and laying it by her feet. Like many Brits, she'd always wanted to visit California but knew little about the deserts or the heat. Thank goodness Thatch's truck had air conditioning.

"Would someone like Professor Whittaker know about this place?" she said.

"Maybe when he was a kid. Could have come out here with his family. You'd be surprised how many dads bring their children to camp and hike in Anza-Borrego Park. There's fishing in the mountains, too, and a lot of ATV off-roading. I used to bring my kids out here on weekends. Nowadays I come to study the geology."

"Alone?"

"Yep. This place is a mystery in itself, and it's an incredible treasure trove for geologists, if you're interested in rocks, of course." He slid a glance toward Tosca. "Which obviously you are."

"Only those in rock gardens," she answered demurely.

He asked her to check the GPS. She read out the numbers.

"Let me see that." He took the unit from her, handed it back, turned right onto the scrubland and parked. He pointed to a low-lying, straggly bush in front of them.

"That's the spot."

They walked over to the bush, Tosca opening her parasol to shield herself from the sun's intense heat.

"No sign of digging," said Thatch. "There wouldn't be, I guess. It was around five years ago, if the forensics tests are correct, so there'd be enough erosion by now to expose anything buried here."

"Wouldn't that depend on how deep something was buried? So what do we do now?" Unable to keep the disappointment from her voice, Tosca walked aimlessly around the site, kicking at the small round boulders at her feet

"Wait a minute, Thatch, aren't these rocks the same kind as Whittaker's?" She bent down and picked one up, passing it over to Thatch.

"Yes," he said, hefting it in his hand. "These are the concretions I told you about. They're found only in one area of this region, right here. Some are cannonball shaped, like this. They're normally resistant to erosion. That's why I was surprised to see the one from the professor's yard had crumbled until I realized it was man-made."

"How did he copy them?"

"It was easy. He used a cement and sand composition to resemble real ones. In fact," he said, kicking one at his feet, "this one is just about the same size as the one you stole."

Grinning, Tosca twirled her parasol and said, "Now look, Thatch, if Paul's hands were inside the professor's man-made concretions, I am as sure as a billy goat there's a clue to the rest of that poor student right here."

Walking farther afield, she closed the parasol with a firm snap and jabbed it several times at random into different parts of the soft sand. Sinking halfway up its length at one place, the parasol suddenly jarred in her hand.

"Thatch, I've hit something!"

"Probably the bones of a jack rabbit."

"Can we dig it up and see?"

"Sure. I've got an old army shovel and a geology kit in the truck. Be right back. You won't faint, will you? I'm right here, *skiansekigyon.*"

Tosca burst out laughing, "You nitwit. That's the male version, the word you say to another man."

"Whatever." He grinned, shrugged and went to retrieve the shovel from the truck. When he returned he said, "You can remove that purple weapon now."

Tosca pulled up the parasol, shook it and opened it up. Sand fell from its folds. She shook it again and held it over her head, grumbling quietly about the searing heat.

As Thatch bent to his task, digging deeper and deeper, she kept up a running commentary of instruction.

"Watch out. You're letting the sand fall back in. Be careful. Goodness me, you're not a very good digger, are you? Aren't you supposed to use a brush?"

"A brush would be great, but I'm a geologist, not an archaeologist, so I don't carry one around, and my rock hammer would be unsuitable. Hey, Tosca, I've hit something."

"What is it, a box? Maybe more music scores with numbers?"

Thatch stopped digging and threw the shovel aside. On his knees, he gently cleared away the sandy soil with his hands, exposing the corner of a tarp and a colorful turquoise beach blanket. Shielding it from Tosca's view with his body, he unwrapped one side of the tarp and blanket carefully, rewrapped the coverings and got to his feet,

"Stand back, Tosca. Don't look."

"What is it? What have you found? A good clue?"

"More than we bargained for. Bones." He walked a distance away from the hole he'd dug. "We need to call the sheriff."

TWENTY-FOUR

For the second time since her arrival in America, Tosca watched a forensics team process the scene of a crime. After Thatch's 911 call notifying the dispatcher of the situation and providing directions, they had waited only twenty minutes before two sheriff's SUVs, an ambulance and the medical examiner's station wagon showed up at the site.

The team got to work quickly, the photographer taking photos, a video cameraman taping the removal of the skeleton, and technicians bagging dirt from the grave and the surrounding area.

Tosca and Thatch stood off to one side with one of the sheriff's deputies, giving their statements.

"See anyone else out here?"

"Not a soul," said Tosca.

"No, officer, said Thatch. "We haven't seen anyone since we left Ramona this morning and turned off onto this trail here."

"You dug this up. How did you happen to do that, sir?"

Thatch explained that the Newport Beach police were investigating a murder on Isabel Island, and one of Tosca's neighbors could have been involved.

"Yes, he's right," Tosca broke in. "We were following a clue to this place. Purely on a whim, officer."

"A clue, ma'am?"

"Yes, indeed. You see, Arnold Schoenberg and Professor Haiden Whittaker have a lot in common. They both love numbers. So we just followed the numbers, and here we are."

Having delivered what she considered a sufficient summary of events that led to the discovery of the grave, she closed her parasol and walked over to the ambulance. The deputy turned his attention back to Thatch.

"Mr. MacAulay, we need you both to come down to our office. The lady's explanation is a little lacking, don't you agree?"

"Yes. I'll be happy to clarify things. It's kind of complicated."

As Thatch continued to talk with the officer, Tosca decided to get as close as possible to the coroner, who appeared to be completing his supervision of the scene. A balding man of middle age, he watched the medical technicians place the skeleton inside a small body bag and onto a gurney. That's all we are at the end, she thought, a bundle of bones. Sure puts things into perspective.

"What a beautiful, interesting desert this is," she said, addressing the coroner. "How fortunate you are to have such a glorious place. I'd be out here every weekend if I could."

"Thank you." He held out his hand. "I am Doctor Daniel Leight, at your service. You are from England, I assume?"

"Yes, Tosca Trevant, here temporarily," said Tosca. "I must say, your Anza-Borrego is nothing like anything we have in England," she said, adding a silent, thank God.

"It's certainly a wild, wonderful area. Too many people feel it's desolate and unfriendly, but I'm glad to hear you appreciate it."

"Indeed, yes," said Tosca, opening her parasol and twirling it flirtatiously, "and I am fascinated with your crime procedures, although there's probably nothing much for you to do here, doctor," said Tosca.

"As a matter of fact, you're right to a certain extent. It will be up to the forensic anthropologist to determine the age, sex, size and race of this person."

"I wonder if you happened to notice anything odd about the arms?"

"Well, yes, although nothing will be confirmed until we're back in the morgue, and I make my formal autopsy report. We have our rules, you know."

"Oh, of course," said Tosca. "I wouldn't dream of asking you to tell me anything you shouldn't, but I was surprised to see when your technician was rewrapping the skeleton that the bones weren't arranged as I'd imagine they'd be. They were almost in a pile."

"That's a common misconception." Leight smiled. "Bodies do not decompose uniformly. That is, parts may not decompose at the same time, so they may not be connected together like a skeleton in a science class. Once the tissues, ligaments and tendons have decayed, you'll often find the bones in completely different places from where they belong."

"Doctor, how interesting. As I said, I was struck by what I imagine are the forearm bones. Would it be possible to take just a peek at them before they go to the morgue?"

Dr. Leight began to shake his head.

"I promise not to touch anything," said Tosca. "My father was a ship's surgeon in the Royal Navy, so I have an interest, you understand."

The coroner told the technicians to roll the gurney back out and unzip the body bag. He pointed to a bone.

"As you can see, Mrs. Trevant, the hand is missing, as it is from the other arm, too. We'll be able to hazard a guess as to how that happened later." The doctor reclosed the bag, and the technician rolled the gurney back into the vehicle. "What's your interest? You obviously have one, and there's a reason for it. Care to tell me?"

Tosca told the coroner, in general terms, of her suspicions, including that the hands had been chopped off after the murder.

"They may have belonged to a music student, but I don't know the motive yet," she said.

"That a disturbing tale. As for a motive, sometimes there's a desire to retain a souvenir," said Dr. Leight, "or no motive except anger or some other strong emotion."

"True," agreed Tosca, "although Henry VIII needed no motive. Whenever he got tired of his wife, he yelled out, 'Next!'"

Dr. Leight laughed. "The police will probably solve the case. Is this your husband?"

He turned toward Thatch as the former agent approached.

"Good heavens, no. Just a friend."

"We can leave now, Tosca. Ready?" said Thatch.

She said goodbye to the doctor. Thatch took her elbow and steered her toward his pickup.

"We need to stop at the police station and sign formal statements," he said. "Then we can go home."

"Fine. I'm ready to get out of this strange place. I can't believe people come to this desert for pleasure."

"Didn't I overhear you saying to the coroner that it was beautiful here?"

At his amused grin Tosca turned away to hide her own smile, then turned back to Thatch.

"I wonder what Haiden will do when he learns we've found Paul Holloway or Monica."

Thatch shook his head. "No confirmation of who it is yet. Could take weeks, and maybe it's someone else entirely."

"Oh! Why didn't I think of that? You mean, the professor may have murdered more than one person?"

"It's obvious the gravesite is connected to him, since we have the coordinates that he wrote on that piece of music. Now leave it up to the police. We're done with it."

TWENTY-FIVE

Professor Whittaker punched in the code on the keypad at the entrance to Gustave Vernays' parking garage and waited for the coin dealer to buzz the gate open. When he reached the penthouse floor, the professor turned to the camera and waved his hand in greeting. The door opened quickly.

"Good evening, Haiden," said Vernays. He was dressed in one of his customary embroidered silk smoking jackets that never failed to annoy the professor as being overly European. "What a nice surprise. Come in. And what a fine evening it is. What can I get you? I have a new red from Chile, just arrived."

Whittaker settled himself as best he could onto what he knew was an uncomfortable sofa, rather than sit on the chair at Vernays' desk as he usually did when he had coins to display or was considering buying. This was to be a simple discussion about the progress of the sale of his collection, which he assumed was safely tucked away in the fence's vault.

"Yes, thanks. That sounds excellent."

Vernays poured them each a glass of wine from a Waterford decanter and sat opposite his client.

"To what do I owe the pleasure? Ah," he said, raising a palm toward Whittaker. "I know. The collection, right? Or have you changed your mind? I have two Celtic currency rings, Bronze Age, that will interest you if you're thinking of adding to your inventory. Or how about an extremely rare Brasher Doubloon? Only seven in the world, you know."

"No, thank you. I told you, I want to sell, not buy, the entire collection. What's happening? Any luck?"

"A few inquiries." Vernays shrugged and fell silent.

"And?" Whittaker prompted.

"There's a… ah… a slight complication." The Swiss took a sip of wine.

"What the hell does that mean?"

"Surely you heard about the death on Isabel Island?"

Whittaker felt his blood pounding. "Of course, but I don't gossip." Not like that Tosca woman, he thought. "So what's that got to do with me and selling my collection?"

"Someone on the island found the body, and near it, almost buried in the sand, was an aegina. I was really excited when the police brought it to me to evaluate. They know my, ah, reputation. Naturally, I recognized it immediately, although I didn't tell them so. Anyway, they got a search warrant and went through the contents of my safe. Don't panic," he told Whittaker, who had risen to his feet. "The police have no idea that the coin was part of your collection. How could they? Your name isn't on it, and you know I don't keep clients' names in my catalogs, not even on a database on my computer."

Whittaker waited.

"After the detective left I checked your collection again. Something interesting has occurred. Your aegina, the one I obtained for you, is not among the coins you left with me, and I know it wasn't in the five envelopes you decided to take with you. Now it appears that the coin is missing."

Whittaker sat down. The silence between the two men stretched out before the professor said, "Impossible. It's so small, I didn't even realize it was gone. Must have been stolen from me long ago. Maybe one of my music students took it. I probably left the tray out by mistake."

"Quite a coincidence, though, don't you agree? Your coin is missing, and it turns up next to a corpse."

"So what? Nothing to do with me."

"Come now, Haiden, it's an aegina. Your aegina. Have you forgotten where you got it?"

"It's not mine, I tell you." Whittaker felt the sweat running down his neck. "It's not the only one in the world, Gustave."

"True, but it's the only one that came from that museum in Australia." The Swiss waved a hand. "Well, let's not quibble. It's no business of mine."

"No, it isn't," said the professor, recovering his equilibrium. "Your business is to sell my collection, and you don't seem to be having much success."

"I'm going to be blunt with you. I've had your collection taken out of the country. I don't plan to put it on the market again until things have quieted down."

"What things? I told you, the murder of that kid has nothing to do with me."

"Nevertheless, I'm not taking any chances. The Greek coin worries me. Sorry, but that's the way it is." Vernays stood up. "Thank you for coming. I believe we understand each other, yes?"

Whittaker realized there was no point in arguing. He knew his collection was safe with the dealer, and eventually it would fetch a good price.

He left and drove back to Isabel Island.

TWENTY-SIX

Tosca walked quickly up and down the length of the street twice before running back into the house, urgently calling out to J.J.

"*A-barth an!* Dammit! My car's been stolen! I parked half a block away yesterday, and it's gone. Gone! You told me this was a very safe neighborhood. I'd better call the police."

Before Tosca could reach the kitchen phone her daughter beat her to it, placing her hand over the receiver.

"What are you doing?" said Tosca. "Would you prefer to call the police yourself? What's the matter, afraid they won't understand me? I don't plan to speak in Cornish, you know."

"Calm down, Mother. I was going to tell you after breakfast. I returned your rental car to the agency after you came home last night. John picked me up and drove me back here. Don't worry, I paid the bill. Here's the receipt." She fished the papers out of her purse.

"Returned it, but why? I need that car. How am I supposed to get around?" Her face turned red at her daughter's smile. "Oh, no you don't. You think you're forcing me to learn that stick shift, aren't you? Well, it won't work. I'll just go and get another rental, that's all."

J.J. shrugged, picked up her purse, took out the keys to the Austin-Healey and jangled them noisily. "I'm leaving these on the table for you. Better yet, I'll put them in here." Opening Tosca's black leather tote bag, she dropped the keys inside and closed the zipper. "I'll drive the Porsche," she added. "Now don't forget, Mother, the reverse gear is to the left and up, and only pull out the choke if it's cold. Gotta run. See you later."

After J.J. left Tosca sat at the dining table, where the file folders on the Whittaker case were spread out. As she pieced together her theory, she went over it several times in her mind. Hell of a feature story. Maybe the *London Daily Post* will run it as a series, she thought, over a period of weeks. Or how about a book? No, that would take too long. The story must appear quickly so she could go home sooner. She could see her new business card: "Tosca Trevant. Investigative Reporter."

As she wrote, the article took on more shape. Monica seduced Paul Holloway. The professor killed him in a jealous rage and chopped off his hands before burying him in the desert. He encased them in fake rocks and placed them in his front garden. Whittaker probably regretted murdering Paul, hence the shrine; but time eroded the cement around one of the skeletal hands, and Paul's fingertips were revealed. Haiden, as Paul's teacher, had access to the boy, which in turn meant he murdered him. But why didn't he kill Monica? The professor's darned lucky she drowned in the hotel swimming pool in Mexico. Otherwise, I'd suspect him of murdering her, too. That leaves the ferry murder to be solved. No, I'll get to that later, she decided.

Convinced she now held all the pieces to the puzzle after spending the afternoon and early evening sorting it out and writing down her findings, Tosca was eager to confront the professor. Can I get him to confess? she wondered. Her knack for dealing with palace staff, reputedly the most closed-mouthed citizens in the United Kingdom, had always proved invaluable in coaxing confidences. Her informants usually responded to her empathy, especially many of the twelve hundred or so permanent members of the various royal households, such as the caterers, housekeepers, media consultants, art curators and strategic planners. The opportunity to gather gossip was endless.

Tosca was expert at sympathizing with harried footmen and maids, offering condolences to trainee butlers and praising sous chefs on their cooking. She tut-tutted when the Lord Chamberlain's Office complained of being overwhelmed with ceremonial events and shared a few belly laughs over beers with off-duty palace guards.

"How amusing," she murmured to herself, reading a clipping from the front page of a newspaper that carried a story on one of the royal chauffeurs being bribed by two undercover British reporters to be admitted clandestinely into the Palace. Goodness, she thought, I've been doing that for years.

Summer months in particular were rewarding for the "Tiara Tittle-tattle" column when extra personnel were recruited to handle the half-million tourists thronging the monarch's massive home. Every August and September, Buckingham Palace's State Rooms were open to the public, and temporary jobs opened up for ticket-takers, supervisors, assistants, wardens and guides. All grist for her gossip mill.

Now, after checking her tape recorder and replacing the batteries with new ones, she was ready to face Haiden. As she was heading to the kitchen, her iPhone rang.

"Hello, Thatch," she said, reading his name onscreen. "Nice of you to call."

"Tosca, just thought I'd let you know that Andy says Vernays has been cleared of the ferry boat kid's murder. Seems he has an airtight alibi. He was at an estate auction in Ohio. The authorities checked his cell phone records. Vernays made a few calls from that location, and his credit card reflects expenses for the hotel bill and other items, too, so he's off the hook."

"Would he have had time to fly back here, then return to Ohio?" said Tosca.

"He was with three other people most of the time, and they corroborate his statement. So that means the killer is still out there, and it could be someone on Isabel Island. I advise you to stay at home tonight because the police are going to hold a press conference at five o'clock to announce they are closing in on a possible suspect.

"Why would they announce that? Won't it warn the murderer to flee?" said Tosca.

"I think they expect to flush him out."

"So who is it?"

"Andy can't tell me who it is, of course, but as you were the one to find the ferry worker's body, you could be in danger.

"But that's all I did, find the body."

"And the coin, don't forget."

Tosca sighed. "Look, there's no reason for the killer to come after me. Besides I'm working on the professor's case, not the ferry killing. Although solving two cases at once would be quite a coup." She paused, then said, "I'd better wrap up the music student's murder first. It has all come together rather nicely. I'm off to Haiden's house now. See you later."

"Tosca! His house? No! Don't…"

Despite Thatch's urgent protest, Tosca broke the connection, eager to be on her way. What cheek that man has, telling me what to do. I'll beat him to the punch, she thought, and I bet I could solve the ferry killing, too, if I weren't so busy with the murder of Paul Holloway.

Mentally hugging herself with delight at the notion and imagining the reaction of her editor in London when she solved the crime, she picked up her last jug of mead. The box she'd sent to J.J. was now empty. She'd hoped the wine would last until she could brew more, but at the rate she'd been doling it out, she was now bereft of her favorite potion. Still, it was worth it if it resulted in an early end to her exile, a triumphant return to England and a well-earned promotion, assuming the lawsuit had been sorted out. She'd miss the glorious weather in California, of course, and the kindness and generosity of Americans, but home beckoned.

She admitted to herself she'd quite changed her attitude toward those she initially thought of as warmongering heathens. Now she could see herself enjoying a whole year on Isabel Island, but it wasn't quite the same. J.J., she knew, felt entirely differently about England and planned to spend the rest of her life in America, but Tosca needed her Cornwall. It was important to her to visit St. Ives, her hometown, even though she disliked the monstrosity called the New Tate Gallery branch recently built there. Fortunately, it was offset by sculptor Barbara Hepworth's magnificent works. Maybe I'll come back here for a vacation. Soon. To see Thatch. If he keeps out of my way until I've solved these crimes.

His admonition to stay home rankled. I know just what he's up to, she told herself. He's looking for some hero-worship from his son and whoever Christine is. So what if he's a former Secret Service agent? I have the very best nose for ferreting out facts and fishing for information. Let's just see who solves these crimes first.

Carrying the mead, the tote bag hanging from her shoulder, Tosca left the cottage and headed to the professor's house. As she approached the residence she paused to listen to the music filling the night air. Through the window she saw him seated at the piano, rapt in his playing, his heavy head dipped toward his chest, his eyes closed. Tosca again was reluctant to disturb him as the strains of Debussy's haunting "Claire de Lune" took her instantly back to a scene from the movie, *Frenchman's Creek,* filmed in Cornwall. As the last notes died away Tosca knocked gently on the door. It took Whittaker a few moments before he opened it. His expression was not welcoming.

"Oh, Haiden, I am so sorry to interrupt your evening, and I did wait until you'd finished playing the Debussy piece. I wonder if I could possibly have a word?"

"I'm sorry, Tosca. I am much too busy."

The abrupt tone and dismissal were nothing new to Tosca. She was a past master at overcoming such resistance. Sensing that nothing short of a shock would gain her entry into his house this time she gave her best rendition of her Cheshire cat smile.

"I'm sorry you are so busy. I thought you, of all people, would want to know that I have figured out who murdered your student, Paul Holloway."

TWENTY-SEVEN

She followed Whittaker inside. A candle glowed in the large brass bowl on the piano, the same bowl she'd seen several times before. This time the candle was plain white, its vanilla fragrance permeating the room. Where did he buy them? Did he collect candles? Each time she visited, the candle burning on his piano was a different color and always lit. Tosca glanced quickly around the walls. The framed composition with its notes and numbers was still missing.

"Where's the Schoenberg piece, professor?" she asked boldly, pointing to the empty spot. "It was hanging right there."

She hummed its first few notes. Whittaker's head whipped around, yet he met her eyes calmly.

"Packed up. I have a buyer for the house, and I'm leaving for Europe."

"Really? Perhaps you'll come and see me in London, or better yet, Cornwall. It's the most wild and romantic part of England. You might meet a pisky there."

Distracted, he said, "Pisky?"

"A Cornish pixie. They can be very inspiring. You've heard of Inglis Gundry, of course?"

"No, Tosca, I have not."

Concealing her irritation at his ignorance because she wanted to distract him further and get him talking about music, and specifically Schoenberg, she said, "I must say, professor, I am most surprised. Gundry is one of Cornwall's most distinguished composers. They say he was inspired by a pisky and wrote fifteen operas. He wasn't born in Cornwall, but his roots were there, and he spoke fluent Cornish. So you've never heard of him?"

Tosca looked around the room for a place to put down the jug of mead. Still littered with books, librettos and CDs, it was as untidy as before. She cleared a space on the low, black lacquered coffee table next to some cellophane envelopes containing gold and silver coins, set down the jug and removed its stopper.

"Let's have a drink," she said, indicating the jug of mead, "and I'll tell you what I have discovered."

Whittaker's dark brown eyes narrowed. God, he's so transparent, she thought. He's acting just like the sociopathic killer he is. Very calm, verging on arrogant, not the flustered man I met on a previous visit. Is this another side of him? Does he have a fetish for fingers, or is he simply a ruthless criminal? He's certainly cold-blooded, cutting off the student's hands; but according to his cousin Betty, Haiden already practiced the morbid act as a child, sawing off animal paws.

"It was the most grisly thing I'd ever seen," Betty had told her on the phone when Tosca had called ostensibly to offer condolences on Monica's death but in reality to dig for details. "Just hacking and chopping at those poor creatures' legs. I don't know if they were already dead or not, because I ran away to tell my dad. Haiden must have hidden them in the barn. We never found out what he did with them."

"At least he didn't eat them, like that cannibalistic Jeffrey Dahmer did when he killed those young men and had their livers for lunch."

Betty hadn't responded. All Tosca heard was a slight gasp. Shocking, indeed, but one must face facts, she had told the woman, who soon made an excuse to say goodbye and hung up.

Now Tosca sat on the sofa as the professor picked up the small but heavy earthenware jug, swung it back and forth as if estimating its weight and said, "I'll get some glasses."

He took the jug with him into the kitchen and returned with two half-filled wineglasses. Tosca peered at the drink he'd set in front of her. Its color was a little lighter than the previous mead she'd brewed. Perhaps she hadn't fermented it long enough. Was that sediment in the bottom of the glass? Next time, she would adjust the recipe.

"So," said Whittaker, sitting down again, "it seems you wish to unburden yourself of some discovery you've made?"

His silky tone and choice of words gave Tosca pause. Why was he so confident? Understandable, perhaps. She'd read that a sociopath has no conscience, that he'll do whatever suits him, as if he is the only one that matters. Calculating and self-centered, yet often extremely talented in the arts. Some, in fact, are geniuses. She really should have studied the criminal mind a lot more than she had, she reflected, instead of reading a few parts of the book she'd bought.

"Well?" demanded the professor, breaking in to her thoughts. "Tell me what's troubling you."

Naturally, she thought, I'm not going to reveal exactly how far along the law enforcement investigation into Holloway's murder has progressed. I'm not that foolish. Still, I'm eager to gauge Whittaker's reaction to my theory. She decided to dangle a few tantalizing morsels.

"Haiden," she said. "I told you already. The finger bones in that huge round stone in your garden belonged to your student, Paul Holloway."

"How can you possibly know that?"

Tosca noted the arrogance and disdain in the professor's voice as he contested her statement.

"It wasn't difficult to figure it out," she said. "I gave the rock to the authorities, and the FBI lab compared them to the other bones."

"Other bones? What other bones?"

"Oh." *A-barth an Jowl!* Damn! That was a slip.

"Umm," she continued, "some other bones were found in the desert, and I guess they matched them up." She fluttered her hands as if shooing away mosquitoes.

"Found where?" said Whittaker, his voice rising.

"You'll have to ask the police that, Haiden. They were a bit vague about it all."

"But you seem to be very well-informed yourself, Tosca. Please elaborate."

"Well, there was DNA, of course." She thought for a moment and fluttered her hands again. "From his bones and teeth. And hair strands. Hair can keep growing after a person is dead, professor."

"How did they match the DNA to Paul? He disappeared five years ago. No one knows where he went. His grandfather is dead, and he had no other relatives."

Tosca avoided an answer to his question, launching instead into a detailed description of how DNA is tested, hoping to cover up her revelation that the grave had been discovered.

"It's not always accurate, of course, but if there's pulp tissue still inside the teeth, it can be extracted and tested."

Whittaker stood up, his bulk looming over her. "It's a simple question to which you appear to know the answer. How was the DNA in the skeleton matched to Paul?"

In for a penny, in for a pound, she decided. I'm going for it.

"The police tracked down the doctor who was treating him for asthma," she said. "He has samples from testing Paul's allergies. Actually, the samples themselves weren't kept, but the report was, and it included his DNA."

Tosca waited for a response. When none came she said, "Those rocks in your garden aren't rocks at all. You know that perfectly well. They are man-made. And those things inside the one that's broken apart you claimed were fossils? They're part of the skeleton we found in the Anza-Borrego desert."

Whittaker stared at her, silent.

Fearing he still didn't understand what she was saying, Tosca went on, "It seems that the police had a warrant to search your garage. Guess what? They found a bag of cement. Tests show it is the same batch as that in your fake rocks."

Did her blush tell him she was making that bit up?

At the professor's continued silence Tosca kept talking, hoping that by telling him more details she'd shock him into a confession. She took a small sip of mead.

"Do sit down, professor. You're giving me a crick in the neck."

He went back to the piano and sat on the bench.

"It all fits," she said. "You killed the student for fooling with your wife. You cut off his hands, covered them in cement and crowned the rock garden with them as homage to his brilliance. There's the DNA, the cement and the motive. So that wraps it up. The murder is laid right at your feet."

To conceal the trembling she suddenly felt at her boldness, she reached for the mead but put the glass down without taking a sip, remembering the last time she'd mucked up the recipe. She'd had a headache for days.

Whittaker leaned forward in his seat, ignoring her accusation. "Do you know the origin of my name, Tosca?" He raised defiant eyes.

She was startled at the change of subject.

"It's Anglo-Saxon," he said. "The word 'wite' means a penalty or punishment and 'aker' means acre, in this case the word for the north or northeast area of a graveyard, where criminals and the indigent were buried. Thus, Whittaker. Ironic, isn't it?" He went to the piano and began playing a sonata. "What would you like to hear?"

Nonplussed at his apparent indifference to her outright accusation that he was a murderer and determined not to let him off the hook, she asked, "So you agree that you did indeed kill your student, cut off his hands and bury his body?"

"I did not kill Paul. I did not," he repeated emphatically, "kill Paul."

"Haiden, you may take me for a gossipy, interfering neighbor, but you cannot dispute the facts. He's in your garden, or at least bits of him were."

"That may well be. I might as well admit it now, but I did not kill him."

"Then who do you think did?"

"Monica."

Tosca gasped. Monica a murderer? Surely not. That bubblehead who cared only for shopping and sex?

"Easy to say when she's not here to defend herself."

"Oh, she's here, all right," said Whittaker, smiling and still playing softly.

"Here? You mean her hands are in the garden, too?" Tosca's thoughts flashed to her London newspaper and a blaring headline: Tosca Trevant Solves Three Murders!

"No, dear lady. No part of Monica is in the garden." Whittaker reached out to the candle and lifted it up. "She's in this bowl. " As he smashed the candle back down, ashes and white pellets spilled over the rim of the bowl and onto the piano keys.

Tosca flinched at Whittaker's sudden violence and the fact that Monica's ashes were being desecrated. She took a deep breath and forced herself to stay calm. Maybe I should have listened to Thatch and stayed home. I really must learn to control my impulses, she thought, yet I don't really feel threatened. Whittaker was believable when he claimed he didn't kill his student. His tone was firm. But if he didn't, what am I left with? That Monica did it? She's dead. Now what?

"How do I know you didn't murder Paul?" said Tosca. "You chopped off his hands. Your cousin told me you killed wild animals and hacked off their paws."

The professor got up from the piano bench and sat down opposite Tosca. He said, "I only took their paws after they were dead. It was nothing."

"You appear to continue the habit to this day."

"No, no," he said. "Paul's were the first human hands I've preserved, but I didn't kill him. How could I? He was my protégé. Brilliant. I would never have harmed him."

"I don't believe you. I think you killed Monica, too. In fact, I've written it all down. The story is going to be in my newspaper. Very soon."

"You think you are so very smart, Tosca, but you are completely, totally wrong."

"Then tell me the truth, Haiden."

Tosca wondered how long she could keep this up. Each revelation and counter-revelation was beginning to tell more and more on her nerves.

"It wasn't difficult at all," he bragged, "at least, not after I was over the shock, had time to think and could focus on what to do. There was my reputation to consider, what was left of it. Monica, of course, was hysterical."

"What happened?" said Tosca, almost on the edge of her seat.

"She called me one afternoon, screaming into the phone. 'Haiden! Something terrible has happened!' She was yelling so loudly I had to hold it away from my ear. She was practically incoherent and kept saying 'Oh God, I don't know what to do.' I told her to calm down and stop crying. She really was annoying me, since I had almost finished composing a sonata. For once, I knew it was going to be excellent after so many failures. But she kept on shouting."

TWENTY-EIGHT

"Haiden, I think he's dead! What shall I do?"

"Who's dead? Did you run someone over?" Whittaker counted the seconds of silence after he asked the questions.

Monica finally answered in that stupid little girl voice she used whenever she didn't want to tell him something she knew would upset him.

"No," she whispered. "It's Paul."

"Paul who?" But he knew. Instantly. The knowledge hit him like a block of concrete, and the familiar molten lava of rage surged through his veins. So she'd gotten her claws into him, too. He felt tears welling in his eyes. His beloved Paul. Whittaker shook his head. Impossible. He couldn't be dead. His genius was just beginning to reach its peak. He was only eighteen and so full of joy and potential. After Paul's latest triumph, winning the Borodin Music Award, the professor had felt like a proud papa. Monica must be mistaken.

"Haiden?"

Jolted back to his wife on the other end of the phone, he said, "Are you drunk?"

He knew his wife's propensity for the bottle. He'd stopped going to the Barracuda Bay Club with her years ago, tired of dragging her, vodka-soaked, away from the bar when she could barely stand up. Made him look like a fool.

He could hear her sniffling. "No, I'm not drunk. Maybe a little. Oh, God, you have to help me."

"What do you mean, dead?"

"He's not breathing."

"Did he fall? Where is he? Where are you?"

"Uh, in a motel. He's in the bed.

Whittaker heard more sniffling and thought, of course the kid was in the bed. Where else would a guy be when in a motel with Monica? Maybe he was just sleeping or in a coma or something. Paul dead was unthinkable. Unimaginable. Terrible. It couldn't be true.

"Did you call 911 or the front desk?"

"No."

"Tell me where you are."

"The Dew Drop Inn."

"Where the hell is that? Never mind, I'll find it. Room number?"

"Sixty four. Around the back of the motel. Oh, Haiden, don't be angry. It's not my fault."

"Stay right there."

Whittaker closed his phone. Not her fault? No, nothing ever was. But what had happened to his beloved student?

No time to think about it. Before getting in the driver's seat, he went to a metal closet at the rear of the garage and removed a large beach blanket and a tarp. If Paul was really dead, he needed to be prepared to deal with the body or, he hoped, to ride to the emergency room.

On the road, Whittaker used the car's navigation system to find the address of the Dew Drop Inn. Driving onto the mainland was easy, but, even following the car's GPS directions, the route was taking longer than expected. Traffic on the northbound freeway was bumper to bumper. Four o'clock in the afternoon wasn't the height of the rush hour, but these days, he thought, it didn't make much difference what time of the day it was. Driving anywhere in the Los Angeles area was miserable.

"Come on. Come on. Move!" he muttered. He considered crossing into the car pool lane, which as usual was almost empty of vehicles, but he'd risk getting pulled over by the California Highway Patrol and wasting time. He could always say he had an emergency. Occasionally, a CHP officer would assist in such situations, leading the way with the motorcycle lights flashing. Yeah, that would be the icing on the cake all right. Step right in, officer. Here's the body.

Finding the motel, the professor drove around to the back of the building and parked. Only two vehicles were outside other rooms, both pickup trucks. As soon as he got out of his car, the door to number sixty-four opened to let him in.

"Tell me exactly what happened, Monica," he said, stepping swiftly into the room and closing the door. Not bothering to greet his wife or comment on her ragged appearance and pale, tear-streaked face, he added, "And spare me the sordid details. You were obviously in the middle of making love."

Haiden walked over to the bed where Paul lay naked. Tears spilled down the professor's face like a river, great splashes that soaked his beard. He sat down next to his student and held his hand, stroking the fingers. Was he really dead? He put his ear to the boy's chest. No heartbeat.

"Jesus, you didn't even cover him up." Whittaker pulled the sheet over the corpse. Then he stood, wiped his face and stared at the body.

Monica squirmed as she sat in the only chair in the small motel room, her dazed eyes averted from the bed as her hands shredded the facial tissues she held.

"I don't exactly know what happened, Haiden," she whispered. "I swear it. One minute we were fine, and the next he was gasping for breath. He asked me to get his asthma inhaler on the nightstand, but it wasn't there. He kept trying to breathe, making awful wheezing noises as if he'd been running. I looked under the bed, but I couldn't find it." Monica paused to wipe her eyes. "I told him I'd drive over to a drugstore and get him another one. I don't know if he heard me because he wasn't wheezing any more, and I thought he was all right. For goodness sake, he was a young kid. How could he be so ill?"

Whittaker tried to keep the look of disgust off his face. He needed her cooperation now. Wouldn't do to have her suddenly take off.

"So?" he said.

"So I got dressed and went over to the motel office to ask the clerk at the front desk if there was a pharmacy nearby. He said there was one four blocks away."

"I suppose the desk guy figured you needed to buy more condoms," said Whittaker.

"Haiden, don't. Please. I bought three different inhalers, since I didn't know which one Paul used, and came back here." Monica's voice sank lower. "The sheets were all twisted up." She shuddered. "He was lying there with his mouth open. His lips were blue, and he looked dead."

"You've paid for the room for the night, I assume?"

"Yes, I paid cash," said Monica without looking at her husband. "So what shall we do? Should we call 911, Haiden?"

"Of course not, you idiot. Do you know what this would mean to my reputation? Not that it's great right now, but Jesus. Orange County's premier composer finds his wife in a sleazy hotel with her student lover, who turns out to be dead. Nice headline."

Breathing heavily as the full impact of the situation hit him once again, Whittaker paced the small room, hands clasped behind his back.

"It'll be dark soon," he said. "Then we'll put him in your car. I don't see any blood, so we don't have to worry about the bed sheets. Wait here while I back your car up to the door."

Obviously, burying Paul somewhere was the best idea, but where? A remote area. The desert was the obvious choice, like Anza-Borrego, where he'd camped with his dad as a kid. Well, he'd figure it out as he drove.   What   a mess. Stupid, stupid Monica.

Tosca hardly dared move as she took a small sip of mead and said, "Go on, Haiden. Tell me the rest of the story. I'm so sorry for your loss but what happened next?"

Puffing alarmingly, afraid he'd have a heart attack, he'd tried to roll Paul's heavy corpse onto the beach blanket and tarp he'd brought but realized he couldn't carry the youth himself. He needed Monica's help. She was much fitter, and it was her fault. She'd have to carry the top half. He'd take the legs. All that tennis she played was finally going to come in handy.

"When I turn him this way," Whittaker instructed Monica, "slip the blanket underneath, then I'll roll him toward you. Oh, come on. The kid's dead. There's no blood. You killed him with your disgusting desires, and now you have to pay for them."

Monica shook her head, still pale and reluctant to approach the bed. "He was dead when I got back." She wiped her eyes.

"Stop whimpering, for God's sake. You brought on his asthma attack. Now grab that beach blanket."

After several minutes of pushing, pulling and wrapping, Paul Holloway was encased in the aquamarine terrycloth shroud and tarp. Not very appropriate for a burial, thought the professor, but the desert was sandy, and the beach towel was fitting enough for the gravesite he had in mind. How was that for irony?

Whittaker picked up the student's clothes and shoes and made a bundle. He found Paul's inhaler, which had fallen into the space between the headboard and the mattress, and told Monica to put it in her purse along with the other inhalers she had bought.

He went into the bathroom, grabbed a towel and returned to the bedroom to wipe off the room surfaces that he assumed Monica and Paul had touched, including the doorknobs, door frames, bedside tables, lamp switches and headboard. In the bathroom he cleaned off the sink and toilet seat, taking care to clean the underside of the seat in case Paul had touched it to lift it up. Next Whittaker checked the small trashcan – empty – and collected two glasses and the large flask Monica carried around with her, usually filled with her flavor-of-the-month vodka.

"I don't suppose either of you got as far as taking a shower?"

When Monica offered no reply, the professor checked the bathtub. Good. They hadn't turned on the faucets. Dry as a bone. The word brought him up short. Bone. Bones. Of course! Good lord, it had been so, so long. The present slipped away, and for a moment he was transported back to his childhood and his uncle's ranch.

How exciting it had been, almost like a revelation. He couldn't remember exactly where the idea came from, but it all made sense somehow. It was as if it was all pre-ordained, that he should be there, that the ranch be exactly as it was with woods and trails and small wild animals. Fanciful, but how thrilling that the reckless, glorious, erotic experiences that summer would be surpassed only when he began composing music.

Whittaker looked at Monica, her face ugly with despair. No, not even the sex he'd initially enjoyed with her could compare with the emotions he'd awakened in himself as a child in his cousin's barn. But that was decades ago. He'd left that strange desire behind, hadn't he?

By ten o'clock there were no other vehicles outside the back parking lot of the Dew Drop. Monica and Whittaker loaded the body, Paul's clothes and shoes, and the bathroom towel into the back of the SUV. He closed the tailgate as quietly as possible.

"Follow me home," the professor instructed. "Stay in the car when we get there."

"Then what?"

He barely heard her question. "Just drive, Monica, and for God's sake don't exceed the speed limit."

"We finally got back to Isabel Island." Whittaker turned toward Tosca, his eyes moist at the memory. "Monica arrived ahead of me. I'd already decided how to proceed from then on."

Monica opened the garage door with the remote, and they slotted their vehicles side by side into the space. Once they had parked and turned their engines off. Whittaker pressed the button on his own remote to close the double door.

"No!" he said, getting out of his car as Monica prepared to exit the Range Rover. "I told you to stay in the car. Move over to the passenger seat."

He watched until she did as he ordered. All right. What did he need to take? Two shovels. Two flashlights. A couple of towels and plastic grocery bags. That should do it. He placed the items on the rear seat of Monica's vehicle, grunting as pulled himself up into the driver's seat and silently cursing the SUV's high doorsill. He pressed the remote to reopen the garage door and began to reverse. Just before pulling all the way out he glanced to the right and saw the hatchet, left by the previous owner, hanging on a nail near the door.

"Of course! How could I forget?"

He stopped the Range Rover, moved the transmission lever into park and slid off the seat. He grabbed the hatchet, still shiny and well sharpened, and threw it onto the rear seat alongside the flashlights and other gear.

"What's that for, Haiden?"

He didn't answer and got back into the car. Luckily, the Range Rover could go almost anywhere off-road. He checked the gas gauge. Almost a full tank. She'd finally got something right, at least.

Tosca held her breath as Professor Whittaker paused, his eyes on the blank space on the wall where the framed piece of music had hung.

"Haiden, surely that's not the end of the story?"

"Of course not. Drink up, Tosca. There's plenty of your mead left."

Before she could reply, his cell phone rang. He excused himself and picked it up. He covered the mouthpiece, told Tosca he needed to take the call privately and went into the kitchen. Tosca immediately stood and switched her wine glass with the professor's. She had read enough mysteries to be suspicious and wasn't taking any chances. She'd barely returned to her seat before Whittaker came back to the living room.

"Sorry about the interruption," he said. "Now where were we? Oh, yes, Paul's burial. Driving to the desert."

TWENTY-NINE

Whittaker headed south on the Interstate 5. Traffic was sporadic, and they made good time to the Highway 78 turnoff.

"Where are we going, Haiden?"

"Never mind. Just sit there and shut up. You've done enough damage for one night."

The road passed through a couple of small towns, where no lights showed, and finally into scrub desert. At the crossroads Whittaker took the right fork onto a county road and followed it as it turned into a narrow, unpaved trail. They passed an abandoned tailings mine and continued driving deep into the desert wastelands, the vague, dark horizon etched by mountain crags against the sky.

"Where are we? Do you know this place?"

Whittaker didn't deign to answer. He did indeed know this place and hated it. His father would bring him to Anza-Borrego State Park every summer during school vacation after he was no longer welcome to stay at his uncle's ranch. He was taught to set up camp and handle a rifle, and he was told to enjoy target shooting. The weather was always sweltering, and he found no beauty in the dry wilderness. The only pleasure he took in their weekends in the monotonous desert was watching his father's face turn purple when his son deliberately missed every designated target.

Driving across the desolate flatlands that were littered in spots with small, round boulders, Whittaker swung the wheel and drove onto a sandy gully. He stopped the car, switched off the lights and pulled on the hand brake.

"Get out."

Monica opened her door and stood outside the car, shivering in the night air.

Whittaker took the flashlights and shovels out of the trunk and handed her a shovel.

"Start digging right near that small bush," he said, waving the beam of his flashlight at a growth of chaparral near the rear of the car.

He followed her and set the two flashlights on the ground, directed toward the bush. He took the second shovel and began scooping out the coarse sandy soil, kicking aside several round rocks. Within minutes he was sweating and was forced to stop. He dropped the shovel, grabbed one of the small towels he'd brought and wiped his face. On the opposite side of the grave Monica paused, too. She had trouble wielding the heavy shovel, and with each load she lifted, almost as much fell back in.

"The sand is too soft here, Haiden. This isn't working." She put down the shovel and sat on the ground, weeping.

"It's fine. You're just not digging deep enough each time. Never mind, I'll do it. Hold the flashlight for me and roll those rocks off to the side. They're in the way."

It took the professor, breathing heavily with the exertion and stopping frequently to rest, almost an hour before he was satisfied the hole was deep enough.

"Come over here and help me get Paul from the car," he said. "Rigor mortis is probably beginning to set in, and then it'll be much more difficult to move him."

"How do you know that, Haiden?"

"One of my students told me."

"How would a music student know something like that?"

"His father was a mortician, and the kid composed funeral music for the services."

They laid the corpse next to the grave.

"Aren't you going to put him in?" said Monica.

"No. Wait a minute." Haiden went to the rear seat of the Range Rover and brought out the plastic bags. In his right hand he carried the hatchet. As he walked toward her, Monica screamed and began running blindly into the darkness of the desert.

Whittaker smirked again at Tosca, then went on. "I said, 'Oh, for God's sake, Monica, come back here. I'm not going to kill you, as worthless as you are. Come back, and you'll see. If you don't come back, you'll die out here. You'll wander around for days. I'm not going to kill you, you idiot, I promise.'"

"What was her reaction?" said Tosca.

"Oh, she came back to the gravesite all right. She had no choice."

"Go on."

"Then what's the hatchet for?" Monica's words came out ragged and halting.

The professor smiled to himself. She's scared out of her wits. Serves her right.

"Nothing. Sit in the car till I call you. No, come here. I need you to hold the flashlight."

Whittaker unwrapped part of the tarp and beach blanket that covered the corpse. Monica watched in silence.

"Damn. Rigor mortis has set in."

The professor placed one of the small towels he'd brought under each of Paul's forearms and, giving two tremendous whacks of the hatchet, quickly chopped off the boy's hands just above the wrist.

Dropping the flashlight, Monica shrank back in horror. "What are you doing? Oh, my God, are you insane?"

Whittaker folded the towels around the severed hands and set them inside the plastic grocery bags. He shoved the arms back inside the blanket and folded the wraps once more around the body.

"Nothing I haven't done before, my dear. I just can't bear to bury these brilliant, brilliant hands. The fingers of a true genius. I must preserve them. Pick up that damned flashlight and shine it over here."

He gestured to his trembling wife to help him, and they rolled the body into the freshly dug grave. Sand was already beginning to fall back in. He picked up a shovel.

"Grab the other shovel," he said. "Hurry up!"

It took little time before the grave was covered. He tamped down the sand. After sweeping the flashlight in a circle around the area, he used his shovel to erase their footprints as they backed over to the car. Still trembling, Monica climbed into the passenger seat of the Range Rover. Her husband closed the tailgate and got into the driver's side.

He started the ignition, drove for ten yards, then drove around in two widening circles, ending facing the grave site. He stopped the vehicle and got back out. Whatever he was going to do, Monica told him she didn't want to know and sat with her head in her arms, still crying.

"But she couldn't resist watching," Whittaker told Tosca, "as I took one of the shovels and erased the tire tracks that led to Paul's burial spot. My footprints, too. Guess she wondered if I'd gone back for Paul's feet."

Whittaker laughed loudly and looked at his guest to see how she was reacting.

"After I got back in the car and started up the engine, I told Monica to find the pen and notebook in the glove compartment. When she had retrieved them, I told her to write down the numbers that were displayed on the GPS unit. After she'd done as I directed, she asked me, 'Why do you need them?' Need what? I said. Of course, I knew exactly how she meant it, but I wanted her to say the words. 'You know,' she said. ' No, Monica, I don't, I told her. Oh, you mean the numbers? The shovels? The flashlights? Tosca, I must admit that I was really enjoying myself. When Monica kept silent, I said, oh, of course. Why didn't I think of that? You mean Paul's hands." Whittaker paused to drink some mead and shook his head. "I told my wife she'd never understand."

Whittaker moved to the piano bench and began playing softly, his eyes closed.

"Haiden. I'm sure you haven't told me everything," said Tosca.

He opened his eyes and rested his hands in his lap but continued to sit at the piano. "That's true. All right. The next day I got up to find that Monica had already left the house. I fixed some breakfast and read the newspaper."

Whittaker went on to tell Tosca there was no mention of a missing student in the news and probably wouldn't be for several days, if then. He knew the grandfather was dead. As Paul's music professor, Whittaker would certainly not report him absent, and his fellow students and teachers at UCI might let a couple of weeks go by before realizing he wasn't attending classes.

"The freedom of college campuses is a benefit indeed."

Tosca made no reply.

"After showering and dressing," he continued, "I went out to the garage to the tall freezer Monica had insisted I buy to hold her bottles of vodka. She'd buy cases at a time, switching between brands and swearing the latest was the best before changing her mind."

The professor described how he had opened the freezer door to check on the toweled bundles on the top shelf. What to do with them? Play-Doh or putty was not an option, of course. He smiled at the memory of his childhood. This time, he told Tosca, he needed something really permanent to preserve the hands that were as precious as trophies. Paul certainly deserved the best.

"I knew they had to be encased in some kind of material, then not boxed and buried or hidden but displayed where I could enjoy seeing them daily and openly."

He told how he wandered out of the garage, through the house, into his front yard and down to the white picket fence, pondering the problem. He stared off into the distance across the bay, hardly noticing the fleet of small training sailboats with young grade-schoolers at the tiller as they coasted by. He strolled to his front door, noted the neglected area in the corner of the garden up against the house and knew he'd found his answer.

"A day later," he said, "I went back to the desert where we'd buried Paul and selected a few of the round boulders we'd kicked aside when we dug the grave. I brought one home because I decided to construct a shrine to my beloved student. I planned to encase Paul's hands in cement to resemble it."

"The shrine is your rock garden," said Tosca.

"Yes. So there you have it. You probably think I am a sociopath or something, right?"

"Perhaps there's something in your family that..."

"Oh, yes, genetics. I've read the books. How could I not when I think of my childhood? My parents were naturally alarmed at my activities, and they took me to for a few sessions with a clinical psychologist. I told the doctor I had a fetish for fingers, but he brushed that aside. I told him about the animal paws I'd put inside the clay and sculpted as animals as a kid. I told him I had no sense of shame doing it."

He stopped to drink some wine before continuing. "The doctor told me I have no conscience, and we had some counseling sessions, but I knew he had no idea how to fix me. Look, I know I have compassion. I recognize beauty. I cry over beautiful music, especially my own. So what does that tell me? Or you? Whether the counseling helped or not, I certainly stopped my interesting hobby, and for most of my adult life that part of me disappeared. But the shock of knowing Paul was dead, of Monica betraying me with my protégé. Well, it all came back."

196

"That's quite a story," said Tosca.

"It was her fault, the asthma attack. Paul was handling it. He had it under control, but Monica, damn her, had to go and seduce him."

Whittaker glanced over at the brass bowl that brimmed over with ashes and shook his head.

"I couldn't afford to have a scandal."

"So you buried him in the Anza Borrego desert."

"Yes, and five years later I killed Monica for causing Paul's death."

The statement was so matter-of-fact, Tosca recoiled. Not a flicker of remorse crossed his face. She struggled to retain her composure.

"So she didn't drown? You sound so emotionless, Haiden. Surely the death of a human being, and one whom you once cared for, shouldn't be so casually dismissed. And why wait five years?"

"She wanted a divorce and threatened me with blackmail."

Tosca shifted in her seat and asked, "How did you kill her?"

"It was easy," he replied. "I remember every single detail. We were having a dinner I had cooked especially for the occasion, and I said something to her that was quite poetic—in fact, profound."

"Yes?" said Tosca. "What was it?"

"I said, we wear our lives like raincoats, Monica, hoping we won't get wet. You, my dear wife, not only got wet, you became totally drenched. In fact, right now you are drowning, or perhaps I should call it something else."

"I'd call that macabre, more than poetic," said Tosca, "but go on."

Whittaker took another sip of mead, licked his lips and settled back as he continued with his story.

THIRTY

He rose from the oak dining table and began clearing the dinner dishes. He carried them to the adjoining kitchen.

"You've hardly touched your food, Monica dear, the first meal we've had together in months," he called over his shoulder, padding about in scuffed suede slippers. "No appetite? Sorry we had to eat so late. What time is it?" He looked at his wristwatch. "Eight o'clock. Right on schedule." He emptied the remains of their lobster dinner into the trash can under the sink.

"What are you babbling about?" said Monica. Raising her voice, she added, "For God's sake stop scraping those plates. You'll scratch the pattern off them. Just stack them in the dishwasher."

He heard her fiddling with the crystal salt and pepper set they'd bought twelve years ago on their honeymoon in Paris.

"Haiden, the only thing we have to talk about now is the divorce. The sooner, the better, right?"

Ignoring her question, Whittaker finished loading the dishwasher and closed its door. He walked past his wife to the front of the room and paused to look out the wide, floor-to-ceiling windows. As usual, the mallard ducks were dodging the three-car ferry on its short run across the bay to the peninsula. At the sound of a car engine he glanced down the street where J.J. was parking her Porsche. What was it J.J. had told Monica? That her mother Tosca, a gossip columnist from London, was coming in a few days for a visit? Odd name but probably not the kind of busybody the islanders would appreciate.

The professor turned away from the window and back toward Monica.

"I am babbling about revenge, darling. Sweet revenge and poison." Whittaker rolled the word around in his mouth like a rare cognac as he resettled his solid girth into his chair at the table. "An eye for an eye. Then there's that little matter of blackmail you tried to pull on me." He smiled at his young wife, creasing his fleshy jowls into folds that disappeared into his neck. He'd been so attracted to her at first, he remembered, a pretty blonde in her early thirties, whose short skirts revealed shapely legs and deep cleavage filled out her low-cut blouses.

"I'm only claiming what's due me," she said, "including the coin collection you tried to hide. That's not blackmail. My attorney says I am entitled to half of it in the divorce settlement."

"Really?" He refilled her glass. "Drink up. We're celebrating."

"You mean you agree to the settlement? That's a big turnaround."

"We are celebrating the fact that I am finally seeing justice served." He chuckled and raised his glass of burgundy. "That's a pun, of course. I served you a lethal dose of liquid morphine in the creme de menthe you finished earlier. I also added a large amount to your drink after lunch. I wanted to test it, to see if you could taste the difference. Obviously not, but I did notice you canceled your tennis lesson. I've poisoned you. Very successfully, I must say."

Monica blinked. "Morphine?" she said. "That's a painkiller. You're being ridiculous as usual. What could you possibly know about poison?"

"Enough to see that your breathing is beginning to slow down, and so is your speech. You've been groggy all afternoon, haven't you?"

Monica tilted her head as she looked at him. A small frown wrinkled her forehead "Is this one of your sick jokes, Haiden? I didn't taste anything," she said, fluffing the curls that framed her face. "Sure I feel tired, but it's because I'm coming down with the flu or something. Anyway, you wouldn't have the guts to get rid of me. I know about your secret stash, and I know you're too concerned about your precious reputation to do anything. Professor Passive Civility, that's you. That's why you didn't make a fuss about that thing that happened."

Whittaker shook his head in feigned disbelief and got to his feet again. "Thing? Dearest, your vocabulary is sadly lacking."

Monica raised a hand toward her eyes, but it missed its mark and fell listlessly to her lap. He saw shock on her face as she realized she was losing control over her limbs. She tried to stand up, but her legs gave way. She fell back into the chair.

"Ah, excellent," her husband murmured. This was the first time since the Paul episode that the professor had seen his wife frightened. It was interesting to observe the actual process of a human being in the death throes. It reminded him of his cousin's pony when they were kids. It had taken a week to die. Monica, he knew, would succumb much more quickly—within the hour, in fact.

The professor was brought back abruptly to the present by his wife's voice. "Haiden, for God's sake, what have you done?" Her words became slurred. "You, you…can keep…the coins."

Whittaker reached over and put out a hand to catch his wife as she slipped sideways. He arranged her limp arms and legs to an upright position on the chair.

"Sit still, dear. It won't be much longer." He took a small vial from his pocket. "I didn't even use half of it," he said, shaking the container's liquid contents. "I have to admit I feel quite clever. The morphine, which you so agreeably drank, causes complete paralysis of the body's respiratory system. I looked it up. Frankly, I'm surprised if you feel anything at all right now." He bent toward Monica, his face inches from hers. "Seven drops of blue liquid that can't be seen by the naked eye if mixed with a green or blue drink. I'm so glad you like liqueurs. Alcohol makes poison work much faster, I have learned. Didn't you wonder why I so lovingly chose your favorite creme de menthe? Of course you didn't. Don't worry, darling, at least the drug is easing your breathing, and you'll soon be in a comfortable coma. Then your organs will shut down one by one and will cease to function. Are your muscles still twitching? That would be uncivil, I will admit."

Returning to the dishwasher, Whittaker set their two glasses in the top tray, closed and latched the door and turned the knob to Normal Wash.

At a faint, choking cry, he turned slowly around, an expression of hopeful anticipation on his face. Monica's forehead rested on the table, her arms hanging straight down. He saw that her mouth was frozen open, a small pile of brownish-white vomit on the yellow plastic place mat. She no longer breathed. Whittaker grabbed her hair, savagely pulled her head back, studied her dead eyes, and dropped her head back onto the table. He nodded in satisfaction.

"Cardiac arrest. Very good." He paced, hands clasped behind his back, every now and then turning to address his wife. "It's amazing how little revenge can cost, isn't it, sweetheart? Righteous slaughter, I believe, is the correct term."

Whittaker walked over to the baby grand piano against the living room's west wall and launched into Chopin's "Funeral March" sonata.

"I suppose you'll accuse me of being predictable for playing this piece, dearest, and you'd be right," he said, turning his head slightly over his shoulder toward his dead wife. "Dull, fat old Professor Haiden Whittaker, lost in his music. Never gets excited about much and can't even come up with anything more original to speed you across the River Styx than this poorly conceived sonata. Chopin must have been homesick for Poland when he wrote it." He stopped playing and closed the piano lid over the keys. "Well, you're certainly not worth one of my own compositions, my dear. You never were."

Whittaker stopped his recitation and looked at Tosca. "That's it. End of story."

"No, not quite the end of the story, Haiden. You haven't explained Monica's fake drowning in Mexico."

A smile lit his face. "Ah, yes. My meticulous planning took care of that. Here's what happened. After I finished playing the 'Funeral March,' I went over to the dining table to check on her again. She was still slumped in the chair. I wanted to tell her that I'd bought a pair of garden shears, but of course, she was dead. Did you know, Tosca, that pathologists use them during autopsies to cut through the rib cage?"

Tosca kept her gaze on him, not answering.

"All right. I'll tell you the details you seem intent on knowing."

THIRTY-ONE

After changing Monica out of her dress and underwear and into one of her red bikinis, no need for shoes, the professor half-carried, half-dragged her body to the garage. He had already prepared the Range Rover trunk by spreading a tarp over the floor. He placed her carefully on top, pulled the sides of the tarp around to cover her and topped it off with a pile of blankets. Puffing with exertion, he pulled down the car's tailgate.

As he walked to the front of the car Whittaker paused to stare through the side window to make sure the bundle could not be perceived as a body by anyone driving alongside. He checked that his overnight bag was on the back seat. Satisfied, he heaved his bulk into the driver's seat, turned on the ignition, pressed the garage door opener and backed out into the alley behind his house.

The professor pressed the button on the device again to close the garage door and headed for the island's main street. Then he speeded up. He figured he needed to reach the hotel in Mexico within two to three hours, since that would probably be the time rigor mortis would begin to set in.

Whittaker estimated the drive south on the Interstate 5 to Tijuana would take just under two hours. It would provide plenty of time to listen to a few of his own compositions, written many years earlier. He slipped the CD into the player in the dashboard, relaxed his shoulders and let the opening bars of the concerto wash over him. It had all gone so well, he told himself.

All he had to do was find that hotel again, eighteen miles farther south of the Mexican border. He'd researched the funeral home, too, and found what he needed in Tijuana, which meant a stop on the way back. Steering with one hand, he took out his wallet, opened it and removed the bundle of money. He laid it on the passenger seat. Five thousand bucks. Should be plenty. He wouldn't need a coffin; a brass urn would look elegant on the piano. He'd read that seven hundred fifty dollars would cover the average Mexican funeral home expenses, including transportation of the body, the cremation and the necessary official documentation. The rest of his money would cover the bribes.

"I crossed the border as usual. We'd never been stopped going through," he told Tosca. "Like everyone else, we'd made several day trips to the Mexican pharmacies. Monica always needed to buy her prescription diet pills there, which were routinely refused by her doctor in Newport Beach."

The professor related that by ten o'clock he'd passed through Tijuana, continuing on the toll road that led to Ensenada. But his goal was closer, he said, San Antonio del Mar, where he already had a hotel reservation for a single night in one of their private villas.

The hotel had the requisite swimming pool, and as he drove up the driveway he could see its aquamarine water glinting under a few flickering candles in lanterns hung around the perimeter.

"Good evening, senor, *buen venidos,"* said the hotel clerk. "It's good to see you back here again so soon. I have the villa you asked for, but we have a larger one available since this time you said you were bringing your wife. We have plenty of suites. It's really quiet this week. The economy, you know."

"No, thank you. I'd like the same one," said Whittaker, "and since we may have to leave very early in the morning, I'm paying cash in advance."

The hotel manager looked at the wall clock. "I am so sorry you can't stay longer. You won't be with us for more than a few hours, then, but we will make you both as comfortable as possible."

"Thank you. I told my wife so much about this place, so in spite of the late hour we will probably take a swim. She's napping in the car right now, but she wants to swim, and I like to sit in the spa. The pool is still open, is that correct?" He was assured that the pool and the hot tub were open to guests all night, but no lifeguard would be on duty until seven the next morning.

A week earlier Whittaker had picked out the most secluded villa next to the pool. Now familiar with the narrow driveway to its private entrance, he drove through the thick canopy of tropical trees and bushes, parked, retrieved his bag from the back seat, opened the cottage door and went straight to the front window to check out the pool.

An elderly couple, arms around each other, red beach towels covering their bodies, walked toward the exit gate and disappeared into the garden. No one else was swimming. The professor grunted and turned to the bed. He opened his overnight bag, stripped off his clothes and put on a new pair of swim trunks. He went back to the car, looked around to ensure privacy, pulled Monica's body from the car and carried it to the pool."

Whittaker stopped talking, as if waiting for applause, then continued. "After the hotel manager got over the shock, called the medics and arranged to deliver my wife's body to the funeral home of my choice in Tijuana, I had her cremated there and brought her ashes home."

He reached over to the coffee table and picked up one of the plastic envelopes containing part of his coin collection. "We are all disposable," he said, jiggling the envelope. "These are the only things that remain. Even my music has deserted me."

"I don't suppose one of those coins is an aegina, is it?" asked Tosca.

"No, I gave…" he hesitated, then continued. "Well, what does it matter now? I might as well admit it. The kid on the ferry was trying to blackmail me. Tell me, Tosca, what would you have done? Self-preservation is as powerful a motive for murder as jealousy, anger and other passions. But as I said, it doesn't matter now. You can't prove any of what I'm telling you."

"So why are you telling me all this?"

"Vanity, perhaps, or to set you straight because you think you're so clever? Maybe to stop your snooping. Or perhaps because you are a highly intelligent woman who appreciates Schoenberg and loves opera. You think I'm some boring, simple-minded old fuddy-duddy who happens to play well, am I correct? Perhaps what I've told you will change your mind."

In the silence that followed as Tosca sought to come up with an appropriate response, the loud click that signaled the end of the cassette tape in her tote bag sounded like a thunderclap. Whittaker's face turned bright red. He jumped up, knocking over the coffee table and sending the wine glasses to the floor.

THIRTY-TWO

"Give me that tape recorder!"

Tosca grabbed her tote bag, rushed to the front door, threw it open and ran down the path. She found the gate handle, hastened through and slammed the gate behind her. To her dismay, Whittaker was almost at her heels.

She headed for home, running. The professor attempted to keep up. What to do? she thought. Call 911, of course. Fumbling in her purse, she found the iPhone. She looked down to dial, but that brief moment took her attention, and she tripped on the sidewalk. The phone went flying out of her hand.

Kawgh ki! Maybe I should bang on a neighbor's door, she thought. No, it'll be quicker to drive to the police station up the road. Oh, fiddle, J.J.'s returned my rental car. That leaves the Austin-Healey. Tosca jerked her head around to see the professor abandon his pursuit and hurry back to his house. Damn, he's figured out I'm headed for the garage.

She entered, turned on the light, found the car keys J.J. left in her tote bag and slid onto the driver's seat of the small sports car. She pressed the garage door opener. In the night air she could hear the professor's Jaguar growl. Where's the ignition? Did J.J. say something about a choke? And where the heck is it?

She located it, pulled on the knob, pushed in the starter button, stomped on the clutch and jammed the stick shift to the right. She carefully eased up on the clutch and down on the gas pedal, just as J.J. had directed her, waiting for the moment when the two were synchronized so she could back out.

Feeling the correct tension, Tosca pressed down hard on the accelerator. The Healey leapt forward, crashing into the rear wall of the garage and stalling. *Kawgh ki!* Wasn't that the reverse gear? What did I do wrong? Squeezing her eyes closed to think, she remembered J.J. telling her the shift pattern on the 1953 BN1 model was unusual. She stared at the controls and quickly re-started the engine, put her feet on the clutch and gas pedal again, eased the shifter to the left and up, and cautiously backed the car into the alley.

After she straightened the car she checked the rearview mirror. Damn. The professor's Range Rover was bearing down on her. Tosca panicked, grabbed the stick shift to slot it into any gear and hit third. The result was a roar loud enough to wake the dead as the car shot forward like a winning horse in the Derby. It was midnight, and the streets were deserted, but she was sure she'd hear about the noise from the neighbors in the morning, assuming she was still alive and not killed either by Whittaker or the Austin-Healey. The little car bucked and almost stalled out again as Tosca tried to cope with the unfamiliar gear, but she managed to keep going.

Gripping the steering wheel hard, right foot on the throttle and now too unnerved to try any more shifting maneuvers, she headed for the bridge. Once over it she'd be safe. The local police station was a straight shot up the hill, a mile inland. She didn't want to think about how she'd stop the car and hoped she wouldn't have to ram the police station itself to come to a halt.

Suddenly the blinding headlights from Whittaker's SUV once more filled the sports car's mirror. She was halfway over the bridge, but the professor was inches from her rear bumper. More speed! Cursing in Cornish, she lifted her left foot, stamped hard on the clutch, forgot to ease off the gas pedal and came to an abrupt, screeching halt as the car once again stalled. The Range Rover rear-ended her with a jolt. Feeling horribly exposed in the little open-top Healey, she leapt out as Whittaker, also out of his car, came toward her with a tire iron in his hand.

He stopped abruptly when flashing blue and red lights appeared on the bridge in front of them, a police siren wailing. The cavalry has arrived, Tosca realized. Within seconds two official cars blocked both traffic lanes at the mainland entrance to the narrow bridge. Tosca ran toward the vehicles. Four cops emerged, joined by Thatch. He swept her up in his arms then quickly released her, glancing around, Tosca guessed, to see if anyone had noticed.

"Don't be embarrassed, *skiansekigyon,*" she whispered in his ear as she clung to him, "although it would have been much more fun if you'd brought a posse."

"This is serious, Tosca. Andy called me, said the cops were on their way to arrest Whittaker for murder. Thank God we got here in time. Took a while to wake up a judge, but they have the warrant."

As he spoke, they saw the Range Rover squeal into reverse, the professor's frantic three-point turn taking him back toward his street.

"He's getting away!" Tosca yelled.

One of the cops said, "No chance. He can't get off the island now. We've got the bridge covered, and it's past midnight, which means the ferry has stopped running. I don't believe that fat fella is up to stealing a boat and rowing across to the peninsula." Turning to his partner he said, "Okay, Bernie, let's go get him. Looks like he's headed home. Thatch, why don't you see if you can move that toy out of our way?" He pointed to the Austin-Healey "We'll follow you."

Tosca smiled to herself. Thank goodness J.J. wasn't here. She'd have his ears for that remark. The police returned to their squad cars as Thatch guided Tosca to the passenger seat of the Austin-Healey. He started up the engine and ran it till it purred. Smoothly shifting gears, he backed the car off the bridge, turned, waited until the squad cars were behind him and made his way to the island.

"Why was he chasing you?" asked Thatch.

"Oh," she said, waving her hand airily, "I was just chatting with him when…"

"You told him everything we found out, didn't you? You went to see him when I told you not to." Thatch's interruption made her squirm. "You could have been killed!"

"It was just a neighborly visit, and I have his confession to the two murders on tape." She smiled at Thatch's stunned expression. "I always carry the recorder in my purse. Force of habit."

"Two murders?" said Thatch, driving down Isabel Island's dark streets to Tosca's house. "It's just one, Tosca. He killed the student, Paul Holloway."

"Oh, no, you've got it all wrong, *skianekigyon.* Paul died a natural death."

"What? But he was mutilated. We have his skeleton, the hands."

"Yes, but Haiden took them only after Paul suffered a fatal asthma attack. Just before he buried him the professor reverted to his childhood penchant for keeping a souvenir. That's a common practice for sociopaths. They like to keep a memento of their victims, although in this case it was quite different. Haiden took Paul's hands because of his brilliance. In Haiden's opinion Paul wasn't his victim. He was Monica's victim, so Haiden killed her in revenge, and he killed Todd in anger for trying to blackmail him."

"So you're telling me that the professor admitted to killing his wife and the ferry boat kid?"

"Yes, indeed. I told you, I have it all on tape. Haiden took great delight in describing both murders to me. He was very proud of himself. He's the ultimate narcissist."

Thatch parked in J.J.'s garage and, with Tosca in tow, walked over to Whittaker's house, where three police cars were at the curb. In the living room they found the professor seated at the piano, playing softly, looking out at the night, ignoring everyone. Four Newport Beach police surrounded him. One was Detective Wally Parnell.

"You might as well hear this," said Parnell. He turned toward Thatch and Tosca. "Haiden Whittaker has agreed to tell us what he's been doing, including tonight's little escapade when he tried to run you down, Mrs. Trevant. He knows you recorded his conversation."

"What's the actual charge?" said Thatch.

"We figure one count of murder for Paul Holloway. We've told him the evidence against him is overwhelming."

Haiden, playing softly, cocked his head to one side, smiled at Tosca and shrugged.

"One!" said Tosca, turning to Detective Parnell. "No, no. I've just told Thatch. You're all barking up the wrong tree. It's two murders, and neither one of them is Paul Holloway's. Haiden didn't kill that student. He died of natural causes. He had a fatal asthma attack. I have Haiden's confession. Here," she said, handing the tape recorder to Parnell.

The police exchanged glances. Whittaker continued playing for a few seconds, a wine glass close by, before hitting a sudden, jarring chord and lifting his fingers from the keys.

"Tosca is correct," he said, sipping his drink. "She does have my confession on tape. Why not?" He shrugged. "I'm burned out. The music has fled. But keep asking your questions, detective. I am adept at playing and talking at the same time. I am a professor, after all."

Tosca faced him and recognized the mead he was drinking. The liquid was discolored and the glass almost empty.

"Where were we?" said Whittaker. "Ah, yes. I may as well tell you what I told Tosca. After we buried poor Paul in the desert, Monica and I returned home with his hands. I brought one of those round boulders back with me and copied their contours using cement and sand. I molded them with Monica's steel kitchen bowls, not that she ever used them."

"But your fake rocks were pink, not gray concrete," said Parnell.

"Yes, indeed. I'm quite proud of that. You can find anything on the Internet these days. All I had to do was Google how to color concrete. So I went to a home store and bought some pigment," said Whittaker. "That's how I created the shrine Mrs. Trevant discovered in my front yard." He appeared to puff with pride as he talked. "After Paul died, life with Monica continued almost as usual for a few years. We never discussed what had happened, but she turned into a bigger drunk than ever. I finally had enough, and when she broached the issue of a divorce and tried to blackmail me, it was the last straw."

"Not good reasons for murder, sir," said Parnell.

"Really? She also threatened to go to the police and tell them I buried Paul in the desert. During one of her more sober moments, and there weren't many, she'd finally figured out that the asthma attack wasn't murder, although there might have been some punishment for concealing a body. Besides, as I keep saying, I had my reputation to consider."

"So you decided to kill her because she threatened you?" said Parnell.

"Yes, but it wasn't only about Paul. There was the blackmail. She found the secret safe where I kept my coin collection. She said she hired a locksmith to open it while I was away at a music convention. She took a few coins to a numismatist, and he told her one had been reported stolen. Afraid he'd call the police, Monica told me she ran out of the store. That's what she held over my head. I had to get rid of her, didn't I?"

Whittaker drained the glass. He appeared totally oblivious to the predicament he was in, reciting his confession once more in a flat, matter-of-fact tone.

The homicide detective shifted in his seat and said, "We need to take possession of that coin collection, professor. Would you get it, please?"

"Sorry, detective. I no longer have it. It's been sold, bought by a true collector, a private party who appreciates its value."

"Who?"

"I doubt you'll be able to track it down. It may have been resold or split up by now and in Japan or Brazil."

"Who arranged the sale?"

"I may be a murderer, but I am not a snitch, and you won't find the proceeds in my bank account, of course." Whittaker turned back to the piano and resumed playing.

"All right. And the boy from the ferry? You admitted to Mrs. Trevant that you killed him?"

"The coins again. I gave him one from my collection by mistake when I was paying the fare. When I asked for it back, he got cute and threatened to blackmail me. The tire iron I hit him with is in my car."

"Sir, we need to take you to the station."

After they left with Whittaker in handcuffs, Tosca bade a quick goodbye to Thatch, went home and spent the next two hours writing the final version of her newspaper story, detailing the part she'd played in it. She emailed it to Stuart in London, warning him that if he didn't run it, she'd offer it to the *National Enquirer* for a far greater fee. She also demanded that her byline read, "Tosca Trevant, Crime Reporter."

THIRTY-THREE

Gustave Vernays, an early riser, heard of Professor Whittaker's arrest on the local 6:00 a.m. radio newscast. According to the reporter, the UCI professor and famed composer was charged with two murders, those of his wife Monica and the youth who had worked as a fare-taker on the Isabel Island ferry.

Reports of the case were on every local and national TV channel. News helicopters hovered over UC Irvine's sprawling campus. There were also overhead close-ups of Isabel Island and the professor's house, plus sweeping panoramas of the bay and harbor with choppers zooming in on the biggest and most luxurious yachts.

"I knew it," Vernays muttered. "I felt it in my bones. The aegina, of course. Foolish man. He should have let it go. He had hundreds of other coins in the collection. It was rare, of course, but not one of the best."

After pouring himself another cup of coffee he sat down at his desk. The matter would require serious thought. He went over the two meetings he'd had with Whittaker, the first when the coin collection had been left with him and the second when the professor had shown up unexpectedly at his home.

During each of the visits the professor hadn't indicated he'd told anyone about the transaction he wanted Vernays to handle. Will the police check my phone bill and come up with my name and number, he wondered? Definitely. Then there was that earlier visit from Detective Parnell, when he brought the Greek coin for me to evaluate. Oh, yes, the cop would be back.

But what could he prove? There was no written agreement with the professor to sell the collection, and no one knew that Whittaker had left it with him, taking home only the five envelopes. The security videotape that showed Whittaker's two visits, the first holding an attaché case, had been replaced. Vernays instinctively rubbed his thin hands together. The police and Interpol knew he was a coin dealer, he reflected, but could the police prove the professor had given the collection to Gustave to sell? If not, this could be a fantastic windfall unless the man was acquitted. Not likely. What a shame the professor had taken those five envelopes back.

As he faced Detective Parnell Vernays found that the questions turned out to be easily handled.

"There has to be some tie-in with the Greek coin found near the boy's body and Professor Whittaker's collection," Parnell began. "Any idea what it might be?"

Vernays spread his hands and shrugged. "None at all."

"We know he spoke to you at least twice."

"Oh, yes. We talked, detective, because he'd been referred to me. He wanted to start a coin collection. I knew of Professor Whittaker, of course, as an Orange County celebrity, a composer and teacher at UC Irvine. Since I pride myself on being an expert in my profession, I promised to contact him when I had some pieces I thought he could begin with."

"When did you make that particular contact?"

"I didn't," said Vernays. "There was nothing I'd have felt comfortable recommending to a first-time collector. My items are for serious collectors. But I suppose his eagerness overcame his patience, and he called me again, asking if he could visit. He wanted to view some of my coins."

"When was that? What date?"

"Sometime last month. I didn't note the date since it was just an appointment to give him some advice. I recommended a couple of books for him to read."

How easily these lies slip off my tongue, thought Vernays. Then he remembered the five other envelopes Whittaker had taken away with him. He quickly added, "Of course, Detective, he could have bought some coins elsewhere. Probably did, in fact. He was tremendously keen on becoming a collector."

"And the second time he came to see you?" said Parnell.

"A few days later. He was really anxious to buy something, but as I said, I had nothing that a neophyte like the professor should consider starting a collection with."

"I notice you have a security camera outside your front door. Can we see the tape, sir?"

"Alas, it's a small camera with a short tape. It's been taped over several times since the professor came here. The camera is mainly to let me know who's standing outside. I only need a moment to see that person to decide whether to admit them or not."

He watched the detective get to his feet.

"Thank you, Mr. Vernays. We may have more questions at a later date."

THIRTY-FOUR

The evening after Whittaker's arrest Tosca waited for Thatch to arrive to take her out for dinner. With J.J. away at another NASCAR race, she'd be glad to get off Isabel Island for a while, but she was still irked at not solving what she had convinced herself was the music student's murder. Natural causes, indeed. Well, she could console herself, knowing she'd helped to bring a killer to justice. If it hadn't been for her snooping, Professor Haiden Whittaker would have got away with his crimes. She was ready to celebrate, too, the impending suspension of the royal lawsuit. Her editor had emailed her to say he'd pointed out to the palace that the offending writer had safely been reassigned to America, "where she can do no damage."

Thatch arrived at her apartment at seven o'clock and helped Tosca climb into his pickup.

"Where are we going?" asked Tosca.

"To my favorite restaurant in Laguna Beach."

Neither spoke as they drove along Pacific Coast Highway and into South Laguna. Their table was ready, and the maitre d' appeared to take their order. After admiring the view of the ocean, Tosca told Thatch she'd decided it was time to try a Stiegl beer, if they served it. But before he could order the drinks, his phone rang.

"Good God! How? When? Okay. Thanks for the heads-up. You won't believe this," he said, shutting down his phone and turning to Tosca, who was staring at him with eyebrows raised in query. "Andy said that the professor…"

"Has popped his clogs," she cut in. "Oh, sorry," she said at Thatch's expression. "It means he died."

It was Thatch's turn to stare.

"Aside from that weird slang, whatever it is, how did you come to that conclusion? Yep, he's dead all right. They're doing the autopsy now. Are you psychic as well as beautiful?"

Tosca acknowledged the compliment with a nod of the head and a smile.

"No need for an autopsy," she said, "though I know it's required. I've been brewing mead for many years. I know exactly what color it is. Yesterday, when Whittaker was drinking a glass of it, certainly from the jug I had brought him, I noticed the mead had a strange hue. I'd never seen it so dark. I decided something had been added, and I guessed it was the remains of the poison he gave Monica. Although morphine is colorless, it must have reacted somehow with the ingredients in the mead. He told me he hadn't used all of it to kill her."

"We could have stopped him, but you never said a word. Why not?"

"He was playing so beautifully, God rest his soul. You know, Thatch, Schoenberg referred to music as a language in which a musician unconsciously gives himself away. In Haiden's case, that was absolutely true. We caught on to him because of the Schoenberg score on his wall. To me, that clue was a prime example of the professor's hubris, hanging it in plain sight. Or perhaps he unconsciously wanted to be found out. In any event, *re'en jeffo mewl.*"

"That's not a term of endearment, right?"

Tosca laughed. "No. It means bad luck for him."

"I agree with you there, but how do you feel about providing the professor the means with which to kill himself, your mead?"

"*Ass yw henna goky!*"

"Hey! That doesn't sound too friendly."

"Sorry, love. No, I'm calling your question ridiculous. I have no reason to blame myself for the man's suicide. I supplied my superb mead, which he absolutely ruined by adding the morphine. Only a man with no conscience would do a thing like that. So no, I have no regrets."

After dinner the couple drove south on Pacific Coast Highway to Isabel Island, parked and took the ferry to the peninsula. They strolled hand in hand past Whittaker's favorite Thai restaurant and reached the pier, where they leaned against the railing, watching a few lone fishermen with their lines out.

"You know," said Tosca, "I could get to like this place. The people are wonderful, and the climate is the best in the world. Stuart told me I could come home now, but I asked if I can stay for a while. He agreed. Oh! By the way, I want you to know I threw away my wellies."

"Wellies? I missed that part."

"Rain boots."

"Ah. Yes, that's real progress."

"*Skiansekigyon,* may I ask you a very, very personal question?"

"I guess, sure, if it's in English."

Tosca hesitated, then said, "Do you have a wife or an ex-wife named Christine? I heard you mention her when you had to rush off to an emergency."

"She's my daughter. She's in a special home for paranoid schizophrenics." Tosca saw the pain in his eyes. "I don't like to talk about it."

"Why ever not? Why would you hide something like that? I know that fathers hate to think of their children as anything but perfect, but it's not your fault. Surely you realize it can be genetic?"

"To a certain extent, yes. At my wife's funeral one of her distant relatives, who met Christine for the first time and was told of her illness, said that two other members of the family had been schizophrenics, too. So I guess part of it is in the genes. I'll tell you more about her someday. Maybe when you tell me what you discovered in Buckingham

Palace that sent you here. I tried to find out from my friends at Scotland Yard, but no dice."

"I'm not surprised. All right, here's what happened. One of the footmen, who has never steered me wrong before, told me the Duchess of Devonshire's new ball gown had just been delivered from Paris. He said it was dazzling and was hanging up in one of the guest bedrooms. The footman asked if I'd like a peek at it. Of course, I jumped at the chance. It wasn't even close to deadline for my column, so I knew I'd have plenty of time to add a detailed description of the dress. The footman took me upstairs, but just as he was pointing out the door a maid came along, and he rushed away. As soon as the maid passed by and was out of sight, I opened the door I thought the footman had indicated."

"Thought? How could you mistake it?"

"Thatch, Buckingham Palace is immense. It has seven hundred seventy-five rooms. There are hundreds of doors along those mile-long corridors. It's easy to pick the wrong one. Anyway, I went in, expecting to see a sumptuous ball gown and instead," she paused, "I found myself in a small kitchen. There are pantries all over the palace to provide snacks and drinks, and this was probably one of those closest to the Queen's suite. Several bottles of Malvern mineral water, the Queen's favorite, were on a table with their caps off. The prince was using a funnel to add some white powder to each of the bottles. It was obvious that what he was doing was clandestine, his movements were so suspicious."

"Which prince?"

"Sorry, that is one detail I won't reveal. I immediately slammed the door and ran off to call security. What was he adding to the water? A sedative? Poison? I never did find out, of course, but the damage was done for me. The royals didn't want me anywhere near the palace or even in the country, so I was hustled out of town, and here I am."

"Hard to believe they'd send you away. You may have saved the queen's life. "

"Possibly. Maybe I'll ask her to return the favor one day, but they were all in such a state they just wanted to eliminate any suggestion of foul play, and that included getting rid of me as a witness."

"It could also mean they were concerned about your safety. What did you do after you left the palace?" said Thatch.

"Told the editor and wrote the story up, but of course pressure was brought to bear, and the column was suppressed. I'll show you my copy of it so you have something to look forward to."

"I think I have a lot more to look forward to than that," he said, putting his arm around her waist.

They looked across the peninsula at Isabel Island's lights, the twin ferry boats plying back and forth in the peaceful bay, the Harbor Patrol boat coming into view, and a few late-night revelers huddled around lighted fire pits on the sand.

"One more question," said Tosca "What about Whittaker's coin collection?"

"The police can't find it. All they have is the aegina and those five envelopes in his house. They remain in the evidence box until someone, or a museum, can prove a rightful claim to any that were stolen."

"So who gets the rest of it, if it's found? Could be worth millions."

"I doubt it will be found, Tosca, but if it is, and the coins come onto the market, Interpol will check for any stolen goods. I guess Whittaker's cousin could put in a claim. The police suspect Gustave Vernays has the collection or sold it, so it could be anywhere by now. In the end, if Vernays does have it, he's the one who's coming out of this smelling like roses."

"Please, *skiansekigyon,* don't mention flowers. I'm done with gardens."

Letter from a Lonely Outpost: *My dear, dear Reader. Yes, it really is me, here to enthrall you once again with a few tidbits that I can't resist sharing with you... first, I've been mining for gemstones on an Indian reservation, great fun and certainly not anything one can possibly do in England...second, there's a new American craze for describing everything they admire as "sick!" I do hope this bizarre trend did not originate in London...did you all read my article about how I solved two of America's darkest murders?...of course I couldn't take too much credit, but your intrepid reporter also managed to pip the police at the post by letting them know, in the politest English manner possible, that what they thought was yet a third murder was simply a natural death...sad to say I was forced to bring the renowned musician, with whom I had shared many delightful chats about opera, to the gallows...well, not exactly...he had the temerity to add poison to my mead...as you can imagine, dear Reader, I was absolutely horrified...I almost fainted when I realized that he had committed such a heinous crime using my mead...in fact, I must have been so distraught I was unable to let the authorities know in time of his dastardly deed, and the next day he succumbed...destiny, I suppose...I may have to visit the UK soon but can't say why, at the moment...I still enjoy Isabel Island, but I am anxiously awaiting rain, wellies at the ready...*Dyr genes *or, as I usually say, Toodle-oo for now...*

Meet Author Jill Amadio

Jill Amadio has worked as a reporter in England, Spain and Thailand and a crime reporter in the U.S. She is the author and co-author of several biographies, as well as a ghostwriter of fiction, non-fiction, and true crime.

Her book, *Gunther Rall: Luftwaffe Ace and Nato General,* was a bestseller and is now on available for the Kindle and Nook e-book readers.

Originally from St. Ives, Cornwall, the land of mead and piskies, she has lived on both the East and West Coasts of the United States. She presently lives in Dana Point, California.

For more information about Jill and her books, please visit www.JillAmadio.com.

www.ingramcontent.com/pod-product-compliance
Lightning Source LLC
Chambersburg PA
CBHW020541130626
46552CB00012B/89